BOUDAPESTI 3

BOUDAPESTI 3

Desmond Lowden

Holt, Rinehart and Winston
New York

for Bill

First published in the United States of America in 1979
by Holt, Rinehart and Winston, 383 Madison Avenue, New York,
New York 10017.

Library of Congress Cataloging in Publication Data
Lowden, Desmond.
    Boudapesti 3.
    (A Rinehart suspense novel)
    I. Title.
PZ4.L8993Br   [PR6062.088]   823'.9'14   78-13253
ISBN 0-03-044301-6

First American Edition: 1979

Printed in the United States of America
10 9 8 7 6 5 4 3 2 1

1

Martin Raikes had stepped off the plane four hours ago. All around him the sounds were new, the smells new, and the thickness of the growing twilight.

And he sat back in his café chair, trying to slow down, trying to think only the thoughts he wanted to think.

He was in a city he'd never been to before, he told himself, something that always gave him pleasure. He had a sheaf of letters in his pocket from Elpart Productions Inc. And there was the Letter of Agreement in particular, the one that promised him a thousand dollars a week as Supervising Cutter, rising to two thousand for any weeks he spent directing Second Units. More than that, it was a TV Series, a 13-Parter . . . eleven months' work.

In short, the good times were back.

And *that* to Shirley.

Shirley . . . The thoughts he didn't want to think.

She'd come back, he told himself. It was only one of her gestures, even if the biggest so far.

And once again he started to go through the familiar stages.

The first, the why-does-she-have-to-flash-her-silly-tits-around-at-her-age stage.

The second, the wounded pride stage. And, let's face it, shock . . . Because he hadn't seen it coming this time. In all the weeks of rows he hadn't seen there was a man behind it. Because the truth was that he was out of practice nowadays. It hadn't happened in a long while.

And then the third stage, the one that hurt, about the kids. They were too young, he told himself, Pru four years old and Simon two, really to know what was going on. But it wasn't that. It was that Shirley and he had never played this game before, the shuttling-kids-around-like-baggage game. More, they'd promised never to play it.

And yet this morning, back in the house in Chorley Wood, he'd waited until the last possible moment, certain, so certain that Shirley would turn up. But she hadn't. And then he'd had to do the other thing. Take the kids over to his brother Jim's house in Twickenham, and drive on alone to the airport.

And Shirley knew. Knew he'd have to fly to Athens today, knew he couldn't afford to turn down this job, eleven months' work . . . Not now the Industry was in its, what, *third* year of recession? The death of British movies, for God's sake, how long had they been hearing that?

Shirley knew if anyone did. He remembered the days when she'd worked as a Continuity Girl. Not one of your fragile doll-like Continuity Girls who sat apart from the sweat of the studio floor, but your Continuity Girl who sat in the centre and swore. Shirley swore, all right. She was large and strong and very, very sudden. There'd been quite a lot of broken glass in their lives, and quite a few packed suitcases.

I am *not* a milk-machine, *not* a nappy-washing machine, he remembered her shouting, and I do *not* give a fart about Andy farting Pandy.

And yet, put that against the birthday parties she'd arranged for the kids at home. The dresses she'd made for Pru, the cakes, the treasure hunts. And the musical games, playing Mozart and Haydn on the piano, while watching through the window the little girl on the lawn outside . . . And once, sudden silence from the keyboard, Martin had gone in to find her bowed forward, tears streaming down her face.

No, Shirley would come back, he told himself, she'd always come back before. She'd pick up the kids from Jim's house and then bring them on out here to join him.

It was just one of her silly gestures.

Not, he told himself, that there weren't his gestures too.

6

But a time to end all that. They were all getting too old for it, not just the kids, all of them. He came to the same conclusion he'd come to perhaps a hundred times before, and looked up from the café table at the twilight of the square.

Athens. There hadn't been time to think about it before, but now suddenly it was there all around him. The shine, the hard polished shine of buildings that still seemed to hold the heat long after the day had gone. The haze overhead, a solid thing, like clinkers in the sky. And the smells too, bitter Greek tobacco and coffee, old salt fish perhaps and oil. And from somewhere a plain, a hot dry plain.

They seemed to come from the streets below him, these smells, almost as though the city were sloping, tipping over the edge of Europe. There were dark shadows down there, a racket to the back-streets, fist-fights even as buses pulled up with hissing doors. While up here on the square there was a calm, a Diner's Club calm, to the evening. The rows of white filigree'd tables and chairs. The Greeks who sat at them, London or Paris dressed. And behind in air-conditioned windows, the shellfish and red mullet, the massive displays of fruit.

The good times, he told himself again, but with more conviction now . . . Except for the thing he couldn't get used to, that after all the weeks of rowing with Shirley he should now be alone, in a city where no one knew where he was. He realised he had to find someone to talk to. And he didn't think it was going to be here on this square. He'd have to go back towards the Centre, where the tourists were.

But the strange thing was that he did find someone, here on the square, not fifty yards from where he'd sat. A face that at first seemed ghostly, hovering on the edge of his memory, from long, long ago. It was a moment before Martin got over his surprise. But then he realised there must be faces like that in everyone's lives, returning from twenty years back, from school.

And in this case the dark Greek face of the rich boy, the ambassador's son.

Martin went towards him. 'Halkis,' he said. 'Evangelos Halkis.'

The man turned, his face blank. 'Excuse me. I'm very sorry . . .'

One of them had changed.

'Martin Raikes,' Martin said. 'You remember? Grayling's House? School?'

'Martin? *Panagia mou* . . . Of course, but what are you doing here? For Heaven's sake, sit down.'

Martin sat. It was uncanny how little Halkis had changed. Twenty years of wealth, Greek wealth, had preserved his olive skin, his slow strange smile. He was still the boy who had bent the school rules with silk shirts, patterned silk ties and, worse as far as Grayling's House had been concerned, scent.

'Oh, that school.' The man shuddered. 'That English public school. Whenever I think of it now. . . .'

'Yes,' Martin said. 'You could be right.'

'All those bookmakers' sons taking on the manners of the English upper class,' Halkis went on. 'That *obsession* with manners. And I . . . D'you remember, I was that awful little Greek who used to pick his nose? D'you remember that master who stopped the whole class and asked me if I did it at home? What could I answer but, yes?'

Martin nodded. It was one of the few things he did remember. 'And that master,' he said then, 'he went on to ask you what sort of home you lived in. And you said, a palace: I mean that was true, literally true, wasn't it?'

'Of course.' Halkis looked away at the headlights across the square.

'And where d'you live now? Here, in Athens?'

'Yes. I live here and work here.'

'Doing what?'

'Some sort of diplomatic charade.' Halkis shrugged. 'It was considered necessary.'

'And you're married?'

'Yes. That was considered necessary too.'

There was a slight edge to his voice, a slight reproof. And Martin remembered other things from school then. Other little manners, as Halkis would have put it, that the bookmakers' sons had picked up from the upper class.

Halkis turned away. He summoned the waiter over and whispered in low precise Greek. Then, when he turned back, he seemed glad to change the subject. 'But you,' he said. 'As I remember, at Grayling's House you were quite the public school man, quite the hero.'

'Oh, come on.'

'Yes, the hero,' Halkis insisted. 'And all because of your talent for lying down on your stomach and squeezing gently with one finger.'

'Oh, that,' Martin said. 'I'd almost forgotten.'

'One finger on the trigger of a target rifle,' Halkis repeated. 'All those badges you used to have on your Corps uniform. And all those competitions you used to win for us at, where was it, Bisley? I was told you really were an outstanding shot, you were going on to do great things. And did you?' he added, 'go on to do great things?'

'Well, I did shoot through a couple of Bisley meetings,' Martin said. 'The long range stuff, mostly. That's what I really enjoyed. But then . . . I don't know, I let it slip. Let the whole thing slip in fact.'

Halkis raised his eyebrows.

'Look,' Martin said. 'How it was, at that time I was doing all the right things. Wearing the school tie, the dark suit, working in the right office. And then . . . I don't know, I just woke up one morning and decided to quit.'

'Quit? What did you do?'

'I learned to play snooker.'

'Marvellous,' Halkis said. 'Marvellous.'

'I got quite good at snooker. I earned enough money for fags and hamburgers. And to see movies. I really got hooked on movies, used to see five a week.'

'And then?'

'Well, in the end there was only one thing for it. I decided to get into the movie business, the Industry . . .'

He was interrupted by the waiter coming back, by the man leaning across to lay small dishes on the table.

Halkis chose one of them. He offered a fork to Martin with what looked like scampi on the end. '*Paray.*'

Martin ate. 'Delicious,' he said. And it was. Lobster meat, rolled in ginger and fried, as far as he could tell.

'You were talking about the movie business,' Halkis said.

'Yes.' Martin nodded. 'Well, it's a hell of a long story, years in fact, but I'll cut it short. I managed to get myself into a studio, Pinewood that was, in the good old days of Rank starlets and marquees on the lawn. I managed to get myself into the cutting-rooms, and found my way towards a director called Dan Leater. Eventually I cut every single picture Dan made . . . and then he started swinging it for me, finding me little bits and pieces to direct. Until finally it was going to be the big one. The picture that was going to be all mine.'

'And was it successful? This picture of yours?'

Martin leaned back slowly. 'It never got made,' he said. 'That . . . *that* was when the recession came along.'

'Oh, yes, your English recession.' Halkis' face clouded. 'But how long did it last? In the movies?'

'Two-and-a-bit years. It's still going on.'

'*Still* going on? But, for Heaven's sake . . .'

'Oh, it wasn't all that drastic,' Martin said. 'There was only one way to look at it really, back at the beginning. I mean, there wasn't any work, and there wasn't going to be any work. So what we decided to do was rent our house to somebody else, and take off across Europe in our van, picking grapes.'

'We?' Halkis asked.

'My wife and I and one – or was it two kids by then? – I forget.'

'But, didn't your wife mind? I mean, a young family, just going off like that?'

'Shirley? Oh, no.' And to his surprise Martin found he was smiling, for the first time in weeks, about Shirley. Because that had been the good time of their marriage, the really good time. He remembered the closeness of that Volkswagen van, the mist over the vineyards in France and Germany. 'No, Shirley didn't mind . . . Nor the teaching that came afterwards. Because when the grapes ran out, we went into the English-teaching racket for a year.'

And after Germany, Spain. The quack English schools in Barcelona, where Martin had been down on the books as both Oxford *and* Cambridge, and where they'd never let him teach under his real name. Shirley teaching too. That grey-haired Spanish lawyer with the private lessons, the man who'd tried to put his hand up her skirt on page 13 . . . Prepositions . . . *Beehind* . . . *Beetweeen* . . .

Halkis helped himself to food from a dish. 'Grape-picking . . . English-teaching . . .' He smiled slightly. 'But you said for a year. And you said too that the movie recession went on longer, two years.'

'Yes, well then we went back to England, back home,' Martin told him. 'And, I don't know, we did a lot of things . . . Bar-work, a bit of English-teaching . . . And I did some moonlighting too, in the Industry I mean, cutting a few little Commercials that didn't show up on the tax form.'

Halkis shrugged. 'The tax situation must be good,' he said. 'A flight to Athens. A holiday.'

'No,' Martin said. 'No, that's the funny thing.'

'What d'you mean?'

'Well, three weeks ago, when the movie recession still seemed as bad as ever, when nobody I knew was working, I suddenly got this cable from The Coast – from Los Angeles – Dan Leater, this director I was telling you about, he said there was a filmed TV Series waiting for me here in Greece. A 13-Parter . . . Eleven months' work.'

11

'Eleven months?' Halkis whistled. 'So, your wife, she's out here with you too?'

And Martin was caught out. 'No. Shirley, she . . . she's coming later,' he lied. Aware as he did so that Halkis had spotted the lie.

But the man's smooth urbanity carried him over. 'A television series, set against the wine-dark sea,' he said. 'That's very good. Very good indeed.'

'It's more than that, it's miraculous,' Martin said. 'I mean, it's big. They've got Dan Leater down as director, Jake Mallows down as star.'

Halkis' eyes widened. Even he'd heard of Jake Mallows, the man who'd made over eighty movies, who'd changed wives six times, and his alcohol-laden blood twice.

'But, this company?' he asked then, 'the one that's employing you? Is it Greek?'

In answer Martin got the sheaf of Elpart Productions letters from his pocket and handed the first one over.

Halkis' eyes flicked down it.

And then he froze.

Martin didn't understand it.

Halkis was staring at him open-mouthed. As if his thoughts were racing. As if he were putting together everything Martin had told him and seeing it in a new light.

And then, not even that. Because a strange thing happened: Martin's mind went back to Grayling's House again. But to a particular time, an afternoon he suddenly remembered with absolute clarity. A grey afternoon. Halkis sitting alone in a classroom while everyone else was outside. Alone because he was in trouble. Bad trouble. And Martin had helped him. But in doing so there'd been a moment, just a moment, when the rich boy's defences, the silk shirt and the smile, had been stripped away.

And now suddenly, after twenty years, the same thing. As Martin watched, all the man's smoothness, his wealth, disappeared. And in their place . . . he didn't understand this, not one part of it . . . was fear.

12

Real fear. Because then Halkis admitted it too. He started shaking. He tried to speak, twice he tried to speak, and failed. Then he stood up. He put a banknote on the table and raised his right hand.

Away down the pavement headlights flickered. A Rolls Royce silently approached. Halkis ran towards it, and was gone.

Martin just didn't understand it.

All he knew was that it was the letter. He picked it up and read it once again.

ELPART PRODUCTIONS INC.

3001 La Jolla Ave.,	Antonadis 14,
Los Angeles,	Athens,
Calif.	Greece.

July 22 1978.

Dear Mr Raikes,

    Re *your appointment as Supervising Cutter/Second Unit Director on "The Striker" Series. A booking has been made for you on London–Athens Flight BE 076, July 25. Also a booking at the Ariadne Hotel, Athens, for the same night.*

    I look forward to meeting you here at the Production Offices, Antonadis 14, on July 26. A car will call at your hotel at 9.30 am.

Cordially,
(dictated by Dimitri Elegesis
and signed in his absence by)
Lela Kalastiria
Production Secretary

2

Martin went back to the Ariadne Hotel. He went up to his room and placed a call to Jim's house in England, the house where he'd left the kids this morning.

'Jim?'

'Martin? Is that *Martin*?'

'Yes. Phoning from Athens. Look, Jim, have you been watching TV? Or seen an evening paper? I mean, Elpart Productions, are they in the news? Some disaster? The company folding up, or anything?'

'No. What are you talking about?'

'All right, some scandal maybe? Gun-running? White-slaving? Anything like that?'

'Nothing. Martin, what is all this?'

'I don't know,' he said then. And he didn't, he made himself give it up. 'Okay, Jim, that was your starter for ten. And your second question, no conferring, is, how are the kids?'

'I don't understand anything you say.'

'How are the kids?' Martin repeated.

'I don't know.' Jim was huffy. 'All right, I suppose . . . Simon, he found his James Bond car in the end. And Pru, I don't think her toothache was real.'

'So they're all right?'

'Yes. Except that we had a bit of a punch-up earlier on.'

'What about?'

'Nothing really. It's just that our kids, our two, were talking about eventing . . . And Pru, well, she didn't know what it was.'

'What's eventing, Jim?'

'You know. Princess Anne, Mark Phillips, the horse trials thing.'

14

'Oh, I see. And it's, I event, you event, he events, is it?'

There was a pause. And then that old black magic, that old black public school magic crept into Jim's voice. 'Martin, I don't want to carp, but it's after ten o'clock here. So how do we get your two toddlers away from the television?'

'Yes, that's a problem,' Martin said. 'Usually we wait till the Epilogue and turn the gas on gently.'

'We?' Jim said then. *'We?'*

There was another pause, much longer. And finally Martin had to ask the other question, the one he hadn't wanted to ask. 'Shirley,' he said as lightly as he could. 'I don't suppose she's back, is she?'

'No.'

'Hasn't even called round? Thrown one of her big acts? Broken anything?'

'No.'

'Oh.'

'Martin,' Jim said then. 'Look, I told you I'd look after your kids, for a day or two, until . . .'

'And it's very kind of you. Really. Much appreciated.'

'But, when's it going to end? That's what I want to know. I mean, you said Shirley knew you were going to Athens. So, how long?'

'I don't know,' Martin said without thinking. 'Last time it was two weeks.'

'*Last* time?'

That was a mistake.

'For Christ's sake, how many times have there been?'

'I don't know.'

'Well, a couple?'

'Yes, I suppose so.'

'Or more than that?'

'Could be, I suppose.'

'But why?'

'Well, you know, there were times . . . times when we didn't get on.'

'Martin.' Jim sighed, changed direction. 'Martin, look, is it money? I mean, I know things have been a bit rough in the film world for a couple of years.'

'No ... no, it's not money. Really ... I mean, once when she went away, we were quite well off. I was working on a Disney picture, and it was rolling in. In fact, Shirley said we had too much money, that was the trouble. She didn't like the way we were getting.'

'Too *much* money? This is crazy.'

'I don't think so.'

'Martin, your wife walks out, dammit, how many times? And ... and with another man?'

'Oh, probably. Yes. She hates being alone.'

Jim was silent. Then his voice was bullish, Martin could almost see the back of his neck swelling. 'But ... but that can cut both ways, can't it? I mean, have you ...?'

'Man and boy, twenty years before the mast,' Martin said. 'Yes.'

'And, I mean ...'

'For Christ's sake, how d'you want it? Alphabetically?'

There was a low embarrassed whistle. 'Most people's marriages,' Jim said then, 'they ...'

'... Most people's marriages,' Martin cut in, 'they sit in front of the television. Or they sit in front of the television and get pissed.'

'But that's not for you and Shirley,' Jim said. 'You go outdoors. The great outdoor types.'

And he deserved that.

'I don't understand,' Jim said then.

'I'm not sure if I do.'

'But what I *do* understand is, you're sitting in the Greek sunlight, filling yourself with *ouzo* and Christ knows what, and I'm looking after your kids.'

'You're right,' Martin said.

'So what are you going to do about it?'

'I'll tell you. I'm at this hotel, the Ariadne, right now. But in a few days' time, when production gets under way,

16

I'm going to find myself a nice apartment here in Athens. And as soon as Shirley hears about that, you can bet your sweet life she'll be out here with the kids.'

'The kids.' Jim let the silence hang. 'Look, are you sure all this doesn't affect them?'

'I don't know,' Martin said. 'You tell me. They're with you right now. How do they seem?'

'Well, they're barefoot, wild. They're hardly out of nappies and yet they can swear at me in four languages.'

'But they don't know what eventing means,' Martin said. Which was unfair.

But all of it was unfair. And it went on until Jim stopped suddenly, his voice worried. 'Martin, when you rang you were quite worked up about something, weren't you? And it wasn't Shirley. It was something to do with work. That company you're with.'

'Elpart Productions, yes,' Martin said. 'Oh, I don't know really. It's just that I bumped into someone here, and he seemed to think there was something wrong.'

'Wrong?'

'With the set-up. It was when he looked at one of the letters they sent me . . . I don't know. Maybe he knows something I don't. Maybe they're crooks, won't pay.'

But if Elpart Productions were crooks, they were rich crooks, Martin thought later as he looked round at the hotel room. It was large, soft-lit, one of those air-conditioned rooms that seemed to be flying through space. And everything was green, carpet, walls, bedspread, television, everything.

The bathroom was green too, of fat veined marble. There was a bath and shower, no less than eight towels. And on a marble shelf above the basin, small sample bottles of after-shave, shampoo, and cologne.

Martin used all of them. He lay back in the bath, letting the warm scented water get through to him, and he thought of a thousand dollars a week.

The good times were back. And Shirley would be back too. There just had to be an end to gestures.

His gestures too.

Which meant little eighteen-year-old girls like Annie Staedtler.

Fin, Finis . . . The end.

He went back into the bedroom and dressed. Then, as he was passing the television, he switched it on.

And was surprised to hear English.

'I have come here to the Athens Conference just as I said I would,' a voice was saying. 'Because I do not believe in these threats that have been made against me.'

A black African appeared on the screen, tall and dignified in a braided shift. 'I do not believe,' he repeated, 'that this group of so-called White Settlers have the power they say they have. I do not believe they are backed by the amount of white European money they say they are. I detect perfidious Albion at work. A campaign in one of that declining country's declining newspapers to prevent me from putting my nation's point of view . . .'

Martin watched the Greek subtitles flick on and off below the man's face. And he recognised him, Dr Aloysius Grivela, President of the new African State of Kanawe. He'd read about him, and about the White Settlers, in a paper he'd picked up on the plane. It was one of the 'declining' papers the man had talked about. The sort that catered to the wishful thinking of a thousand Surrey householders. The people who recognised the sound of gunfire when they heard it . . . at a safe, safe distance through French windows . . . the eventers.

18

3

The next morning was bright and varnished. The Athens of last night, of shadows and strange smells, was gone. The racket was still there, and the fighting bus-queues, but the whole was now overpainted by sun. It caused businessmen to walk by with newspapers held over their heads. It brought a shine to newly-washed pavements, and the flower stalls were thickets of colour.

Martin sat back in the Elpart Productions car that had called for him. He watched as the streets became dark canyons, became the cold stone respectability of the business section. Then, passing a street sign that said Antonadis, the car went under an archway and came into a wide stone courtyard.

It was grey and cobbled. Pillars surrounded it on three sides, with tall curving windows set in between them. The chauffeur got out. He pointed towards the main entrance, and in halting English said it was an office on the 4th floor, number 427.

Martin went in through revolving doors and found himself in a huge entrance hall. It was dim, there were chipped statues and a flight of wide marbled stairs. And the fourth floor, when he reached it, was dim and marbled too. There was the sound of voices from far away, of footsteps, of doors opening and closing. He walked down a long deserted passage and came to a door marked 427–429. He knocked and went in.

And then he stopped, surprised by the size of the room inside. The ceiling was far above him, dim and painted. The chipped statues were there again, and the tall curving windows he'd seen from outside. There were three of them, casting long strips of sunlight across the marble floor. And away to his left, puny and out of place, were modern office partitions, the chatter of typewriters coming from beyond. He saw he was standing in some sort of outer office. Facing him, far across the floor, was a massive carved desk. And there, sitting in sunlight, a woman talking Greek on a phone.

Martin went towards her. 'Elpart? Is this Elpart Productions?'

She nodded and went back to the phone.

He moved to one side, out of the sunlight. And he could see the grey scripts then, arranged in piles on a table. He could see the Crossplots on the wall behind them, and the Schedules, Casting Notices, and Call Sheets. There was the smell of Roneo ink, of cans of film. It was a long time since he'd smelt those smells, and he had the feeling he was coming home.

The woman put the phone down. She reached for a packet of Rothmans and blew a trumpet of smoke up above her blonde shining head.

'Yes. Elpart Productions,' she repeated. 'And you are . . .?'

'Martin Raikes. I flew in from London last night.'

'Of course. Our Supervising Cutter.' She came towards him smiling, holding out her hand. 'I'm Lela. Lela Kalastiria.'

The name that had been signed on the letter last night. And was it that that had caused Halkis' fear? Looking at her now, Martin couldn't believe it.

Lela was a tall goodlooking woman of about twenty-five. Her blonde hair was dyed, expensively dyed, and set close to her head. Her dress was expensive too, one of those fake military dresses with tiny map pockets and ammunition clips. It had a long pencil-skirt in the Fifties style, and together with her high stiletto heels, it took away from the slight massiveness of her face. She stood close to Martin, the shaft of sunlight behind her, and she was long and slim and pale. A highly paid secretary. No more.

'. . . In the end we decided on the Ariadne,' she was saying. 'It's meant to be quite a good hotel. I hope you like it.'

'It's fine.'

'And you managed to find us all right, even though we don't have our name up on the door?' She pointed. 'It was up there once, but Mr Elegesis had it taken down. He wanted it done again. In gold, of course.'

'Of course,' Martin said.

'He isn't here at the moment, Mr Elegesis. He's very sorry not to welcome you personally, but he had to fly back to the States . . . Trouble, on The Coast.'

'What sort of trouble?'

'Jake Mallows,' she said. 'Big Jake Mallows, star of God knows how many movies, biggest grosser of nineteen-sixty-whatever . . . and now, let's face it, coming downhill, or he wouldn't be doing a TV series like this. Well, Big Jake is sitting in a penthouse suite in LA, tearing up sheets of paper.'

'Like, the script?'

'No. Typing paper. White, it has to be white. He folds it lengthwise like this and this. Then he tears it carefully into strips.

'For God's sake, why?'

She shrugged. 'It's his latest way of staying off the booze.'

'And Elegesis is holding his hand?'

'Mr Elegesis is buying up all the white typing paper he can find on The Coast,' she said. 'He hopes to be back tomorrow or Thursday. But meanwhile he says you should start reading.' She passed him to the table where the scripts were. 'How many d'you want? The first five? The first six?'

Martin took the thick grey wedges of paper she handed to him. They were heavy. 'Does he call himself a producer? Elegesis?' he asked. 'I thought a producer was a man with a pair of scales who threw out any script over four ounces. I mean, what's it work out at nowadays? $20,000 an ounce?'

'This one's more like $40,000 an ounce,' she said. 'Believe me.'

She went to a drawer and got out two large envelopes. She put three scripts into the first one and three into the second. Then she paused. 'Oh, and there were a couple of other things Mr Elegesis wanted you to do. I don't know if you feel like working now, on your first day, but I've got a minute or two to spare.'

'All right,' Martin said. 'Let's go.'

She pressed a button on her desk. 'Katy? Can I switch the phone through for twenty minutes? I've got a customer.' Then she turned back, notebook in hand. 'Letters,' she said. 'A letter to Alpha Studios here about cutting room space. A letter to the Xanthe Cinema Chain about a cinema to view rushes. And a letter to the LIS Color Labs in Saloniki. Shall we start with the Studios?'

Martin nodded.

'So tell me what you want. Three cutting rooms? Four? Good modern Movieolas? A post-synch and dubbing theatre that'll take at least eight tracks? Just say. Money's no object.'

Martin sat down and dictated the three letters. He got them back, neatly typed in Greek, with the words 'dubbing tracks' and 'post-synch loops' intruding strangely in the text. And they made him look up at Lela once again.

Once again she was sitting in the shaft of sunlight. And her Greekness, the hint of dark fuzz on her arms, showed plainly against her dyed blonde hair. But it wasn't just that. It was the harder line of her jaw as she concentrated, the way her body seemed heavier, creasing the tight hobble skirt and showing it for what it was, a wrapper, a pretence from another land. And the sudden feeling he had that, without the high stiletto heels she would stand taller, a darker, more solid woman, unable to be moved. A strange feeling, and he couldn't explain it.

She finished the envelopes, then glanced at her watch. 'The twenty minutes are up, I'm afraid. I'll have to throw

you out. But why don't you ring in again after the siesta?
Round about six? Oh, and I almost forgot. Dan Leater . . .'
   'Dan,' Martin said. 'For Christ's sake, how is he? I
haven't seen him in what, three years?'
   'He's fine. He's away right now, looking at locations in
Rhodes. But about the scripts. Dan said to open a bottle of
wine before you start reading.'
   'Are they that bad?'
   'That bad.' She nodded.

And they were.
   Martin found a small backstreet restaurant not far from
the office. He sat outside it, at an oilcloth covered table in
the sun. He ordered a small metal jug of wine, and he read:

'THE STRIKER'   Episode 1.
FADE IN TO:
1   GREEK FISHING HARBOR. EXT. DAY.
       A small harbor, backed by white store-fronts,
       discos, a boutique or two. It's noon, the water
       bounces back the sun. The boats are mostly
       caiques, painted in the bright colors that haven't
       changed in recorded time. But there's one white
       cabin cruiser, trim, built for speed. *Greek Music
       Over.*
2   DECK OF CABIN CRUISER. EXT. DAY.
       A hatch slides back, and JOSH appears. He is
       45ish, a big man, beaten by wind and spray.
       Beaten a little by the liquor bottle too – last night
       JOSH hung one on. But there's more to JOSH
       than liquor. *WE MOVE IN* on him and see a face
       that can be tough in a tight spot, yet soft when a
       gut-reaction is called for. A face that can be cun-
       ning and yet at times strangely naïve . . .

   . . . Tough yet soft, cunning yet naïve. It was always the

same, Martin thought. Always the same buckshot writing. He read on.

2   (*Contd.*)
       JOSH looks up as a shadow falls across him.
                      JOSH.
       Mary, will you get the hell over to the *cafe-neion* and see if Manoli can fix me up with another bottle of *raki*?
                      MARY.
       Josh, you really think you ought to drink more of that stuff?
       MARY stands on the dockside, a dolly bird with cornsilk hair, whose micro-bikini reveals . . .

It could only get worse. And it did.

In Scene 24 Josh got a phone call from a man with a mid-European accent. A meeting was arranged in a nearby town.

In Scene 26, waiting in the town, Josh was almost run down by a black Cadillac with mud-covered plates.

Martin ordered a second metal jug of wine.

He finished the two jugs and two of the scripts. Then he decided to skip the rest and go back to the Ariadne Hotel. He walked towards the Centre and found himself passing a high curving archway with a cobbled courtyard beyond. There was the street-name Antonadis, the number 14. And he was about to walk on by, when suddenly he realised something.

He only had one envelope in his hand. The other envelope, that contained the first three scripts, he'd left back at the restaurant. And he didn't know if he could find his way back there now. He turned and went in through the archway. He walked in through the main entrance, up the marble stairs, and came to the fourth floor. The outer office was empty. Lela's voice came from somewhere behind the partition. Martin crossed to the table where the scripts were. He picked up replacements for Episodes 1, 2, and 3. Then he looked down.

In the wastepaper basket were the letters to Alpha Studios, LIS Color Labs, and the Xanthe Cinema Chain. Each of them torn in half.

4

Lela came in. She saw the letters in his hand, and for a moment there was anger, a hard Greek anger, in her eyes. Then she recovered. She walked towards him, smoothing down her skirt, and smiling.

'Oh, yes,' she said. 'What a waste of time.'

'Wasn't it, though?' Martin nodded. 'Who the hell tore them up?'

'I did.'

'You did?'

'Yes. Mr Elegesis came on the phone from The Coast. Lots of things have been happening.'

'The phone?' Martin frowned and looked at his watch. 'Look, it's one pm, right? And as I remember it, Los Angeles is nine hours behind us in London. So, say, ten hours behind us here. And you mean, Elpart Productions are still doing business at three in the morning?'

'This sort of business, they are,' she said. 'There's trouble.'

'Trouble?' Then he remembered. 'Jake Mallows sort of trouble, you mean? Sitting in his penthouse tearing up pieces of paper?'

'That's right.'

'Only it's more than that, isn't it? More than some quack cure Mallows has to keep himself off the booze? Look, don't you think I ought to know?'

Her dark eyes never left him. He didn't know the moment when she came to a decision, but she turned to the phone, dialled, and spoke in soft Greek. Then she turned back.

'I'd better take you to see Mr Mavromatis,' she said. 'I'll just ring down for the car.'

Martin wasn't expecting a ten mile drive out of Athens along the coast. He wasn't expecting a villa the size of a hotel. But there it was at the end of a long drive, its white walls, courtyards, archways and towers coming down the side of a slope where pink oleanders grew, and where a river ran.

And the river ran inside the house too, he was amazed to find. At first it was small, a stream set in glass pebbles and leaps, burbling through rooms where Rouaults and Mirós were hung on the walls. But then, in a long dim hall of tinted glass, it widened to form a pool. Slow, brilliant-coloured fish swam there. And at the far end there was a fountain, a fountain of crystal saucers that filled and tipped, making the sound of the sea.

Outside in a sudden blaze of sunlight was the real sound of the sea. There was a red tiled courtyard, with the cries of children and the hiss of waves somewhere below its bright white walls. And another sound that Martin couldn't place at first. Until he saw the kites in the sky, five or six of them, with whirring plastic wings.

Mavromatis sat on a shaded swing seat, sat like a grey crab by the blue water of a pool. He was leaning back, with both his legs spread sideways, and his body was huge. More, it was unashamedly huge. The slate grey suit covered his vast stomach without a crease or a wrinkle. And the soles of his shoes, Martin noticed, were unmarked, startlingly new. It was as if he'd been carried there. As if he'd sat down all his life.

'Mr Raikes? Mr Martin Raikes?' The eyes looked up in some amusement. The whole face was amused, falling in dark massive folds around his nose.

'That's right,' Martin said.

'Take a seat, Mr Raikes.'

Martin and Lela both sat in the shade of an awning. There was a fourth person there too, a woman, coiled on the swing seat next to Mavromatis. She was completely white. White skin, white dress, white hair.

'Would you care for a drink, Mr Raikes? Have anything. Anything you like.'

'Well,' Martin said. 'Just now I was reading scripts and sipping wine.'

'Wine.' Mavromatis' deep rich voice became dreamy. He glanced at the tall glass in his hand. 'Wine's good. Wine's friendly.'

A girl came round the edge of the awning, a dark-haired girl in a yellow towelling suit. It was loose and casual. And she was casual too as she poured wine. It was difficult to tell whether she was a servant or a friend.

Difficult too for Martin to adjust himself to the hard blue Aegean sky as he sipped. Because the wine took him suddenly far away. To Southern Germany, a valley where Shirley and he had once picked grapes, huge farmhouses rising out of the mist like battleships. Except that that was only the first taste. The second took him to somewhere he'd never been before.

'You like the wine?' Mavromatis was watching his face.

'It's magnificent.'

'And what d'you think it is?'

'Well,' Martin tried to remember the names. 'There was Sylvaner, Riesling, Muller-Thürgau ...'

'Those are only the names of grapes,' Mavromatis said. 'You understand, it's not the grape that matters, it's the selection.' He rocked the swing seat gently with one foot.

'Perhaps I'd better tell you who I am,' he said then. 'Obviously I have money. Obviously people come to me with certain projects that need money. And one of these people is Mr Elegesis. I've known him for a long time, and I admire him. Such energy the man has. It amuses me the way his polished shoes dance down onto all the airports of the world, and he *believes* the telephone.' The smile spread once again over his collapsed face. 'But that's not the real reason why I back him.'

He sipped delicately from his glass. 'Not the grape, but the selection of the grape,' he repeated. 'Mr Raikes d'you know what the greatest aphrodisiac of the twentieth century is?'

'No,' Martin said, surprised.

'It's a piece of celluloid, 35 millimetres wide, with small square holes on each side of it,' Mavromatis said. 'It has a strange effect on women. They want to place their images on it. Images created by expert men who, shall we say, all seem to have one thing in common. A complete lack of taste. I'm ashamed to say it's that which attracts me most of all. And the rigidity, the exact ritual of the thing . . . These images I was talking about. And these women who are required to do no more than utter words of extreme banality, while looking corruptible and incorruptible by turns.'

The dark-haired girl reappeared and filled the glasses. She went away. The black insect kites droned on in the sky.

Mavromatis leaned forward. 'But that's not what you want to hear about, is it?'

'No.'

'You're worried because certain letters to film studios and cinema companies have been torn up.'

'Yes.'

'Yes. Naturally you're worried. Naturally. You dictated the letters, and they were torn up.'

Martin nodded.

'So we must talk about a phone call coming from Los Angeles at three in the morning,' Mavromatis said. 'A phone call in which Elegesis, to use his exact words, said that nothing was to be . . . firmed up. Nothing firmed up with studios, theatres, or any other concern, within the next few days. There is to be a short pause. A hiatus.'

'But why?'

'That's the question.' The man turned to the white-haired woman at his side, and pointed. There was a briefcase on the cushions next to her. She opened it, sorted through some papers, and finally came to a magazine, *Variety* magazine.

The woman uncoiled herself and stepped out into the sunlight. And Martin suddenly realised that she was young. Her hair was white, not grey or silver. And her white skin was smooth, without a vein or a mark. She gave Martin the *Variety*, and went back quickly to the swing seat, shrinking once again into the shade.

'Page 87,' Mavromatis said. 'It's marked with a paper-clip.'

Martin found the page in the magazine, and the column that was ringed in pencil. MALLOWS DICKERING 13-PARTER, it said, YET TO FIRM 'STRIKER' START-DATE.

'Tell me, Mr Raikes, d'you know what dickering means?' Mavromatis said the word precisely, with an English intonation.

'Yes.'

'And d'you know also how Jake Mallows dickers?'

'How many ways are there?'

'He's a man of a certain humour.' The smile came again. 'What he does is to leave whisky bottles around his apartment where you can see them. He tips whisky down his shirt-front where you can smell it. He pretends he's on a week-long drunk, and the hell with your picture. And you know why?'

'He wants more money,' Martin said.

'Exactly. A bigger slice of Latin America, a bigger slice of the Far East.' Mavromatis said it as though he saw rich brown earth. 'But he's not going to get them, either of them. You see, Elegesis has contracts that can make him do the picture on roller skates if necessary by the end of next week. And Mallows knows that. It's just a game.'

The dark-haired girl re-appeared and filled Martin's glass. She followed exactly the same path as last time, went through exactly the same motions. The black insect kites whirred on overhead, and Martin had a strange feeling of *déjà vu.*

'But if it's just a game,' he insisted, 'why go round tearing up letters?'

'Ah, yes. Money,' Mavromatis said sadly. 'Now we must talk about money. D'you know anything about it? Have you any idea how European-based pictures are set up nowadays? Tax Shelter Money? Have you heard of that?'

'Well, it's to do with big worldwide corporations, isn't it? Multi-nationals?'

'It is.'

'And these corporations have money tied up in a lot of different countries? I mean, it's tied up, due for each country's tax?'

'Exactly. Due for tax.' Mavromatis nodded. 'So we come to the two words, Tax Shelter. A means whereby money tied up in a certain country – in this case Greece – can be invested in a project that's set up inside Greece – in this case our Television Series – thereby reducing the amount due for Greek tax. And in this case too, it's a very attractive proposition to all parties, because the money in question is very large. Very large indeed.'

The swing seat moved. The white woman reached out for Mavromatis' hand delicately and started stroking it.

'Almost a year ago, Elegesis came to me,' he went on. 'He needed my help to tap that money, you see. And we managed it. We received a first instalment, a small amount. But it was enough to get thirteen scripts written, then to get Jake Mallows' signature on the strength of those scripts, and then to set up provisional deals around the world on the strength of Jake Mallows . . . But provisional deals only . . . Because what we've been waiting for all year. And what we're still waiting for, in fact, is that very . . . large . . . amount.'

The white woman leaned closer to Mavromatis and started unbuttoning his shirt. Martin moved in his chair, stared.

'Mr Raikes, can you look at that amount in the abstract, as an accountant would see it?' the deep brown voice continued. 'Tax Shelter Money . . . If the Corporation invests in us, it means by its very nature that we're down on their tax returns. And of course those returns have to be in by a certain date. A date, if you like, which is the last day that that money exists, before it's swallowed up by tax. D'you see that? D'you see what Jake Mallows is trying to do? Frighten us? Drag us closer and closer to that date?'

The dark-haired girl came from behind the awning again. She stood in front of Martin, but this time she had no bottle. He shook his head, not understanding. She moved on to stand in front of Lela. Lela got up suddenly and went in, back through the tinted glass doors.

'The game, you see? Tearing up letters. Not firming up, as Elegesis calls it,' the voice droned on. 'I'm only trying to tell you it *is* a game, but that you have nothing to worry about. You see, you, Mr Raikes, are already firmed up. You have a letter of engagement that guarantees you eleven months' work, isn't that right? And Dan Leater, he has a letter of engagement too. He's firmed up. And maybe a dozen other people on the unit, the same. But the vast majority, artistes, technicians, front office people, aren't yet firmed up. They're all on option, waiting.'

The dark-haired girl went away towards the swing seat. The black insect kites seemed suddenly huge above her. She reached Mavromatis and the white woman. The white woman reached up towards her. There was the sound of stud-fasteners. A piece of yellow towelling in the shape of an axe-head fell between the dark woman's legs.

The swing seat rattled as Mavromatis laughed. 'Getting old, Mr Raikes. Nowadays, as Elegesis says, we have to firm up very late.'

Martin got to his feet.

'Don't go away,' the voice said. 'Stay to lunch. Have anyone. Anyone you like.'

Martin followed Lela's path towards the tinted glass

doors. He passed the back of the swing seat and nudged it with his foot. 'You old Greek swinger,' he said.

As he looked back he caught just a glimpse of Mavromatis' laugh, the huge mouth, the flash of gold teeth.

5

'He was disgusting,' Lela said. 'Disgusting.'

'Yes.' Martin nodded.

He sat back, holding a large brandy glass in his hand. It was evening once again, and they were sitting in a restaurant on Lykavettos Hill, high above the city.

'And you know why?' she asked. 'You know what it was, don't you?'

'What what was?'

She turned to the lights of Athens below. The streetlights, neons, and then those large flickering squares of light she'd told him were rooftop cinemas. Cinemas, she said, that moved up onto their own rooftops in the summer heat.

She pointed one out now. 'Don't you see? He would have had a showing at the villa last night, a picture.'

'What?'

'A picture with a white-haired woman in it. And a girl wearing that awful towelling costume. Didn't you notice those press-studs? Right from the beginning?'

'No,' he said, 'I didn't.'

'Well, he shows those sort of pictures, two or three every night. Then he re-enacts the ones he likes best. He has actors and actresses out there, a costume department, make-up, everything.'

She shuddered, and Martin was surprised at how strongly she felt. It was that dark Greek side of her again. Perhaps Puritanism. But certainly sunlight, the body . . . instinct as against the mechanical.

'I'm not going back to the office yet,' she said then. 'I should, the calls will be piling up, but I don't care.'

'*Back* to the office?' He glanced at his watch. It was late, nearly 10 p.m. 'How late d'you work, for God's sake?'

'Till one, most nights,' she said. 'So the calls from The Coast can come in. But they give us a long break in the middle of the day.'

'Well, if you're not going back, there's time for another brandy.' Martin signalled the waiter over.

The man came, refilled his glass. But Lela put her hand over hers. She still seemed nervous, upset.

'Have you met a man like him before?' she asked when the waiter had gone. 'In the Industry?'

'Him? Who?'

'Mavromatis.'

'Oh, I don't know,' Martin said. 'Some.' He thought of that dark head leaning back then, the flash of gold teeth, and he smiled.

'You find it funny?'

'A little.'

'And you're married, of course?'

'Yes.'

'Oh, I see.'

'See?' Martin asked. 'What can you see? What can I tell you? That for the first six months of our marriage, every single morning, I had to buy a new egg saucepan on the way to work?'

'A what?'

'An egg saucepan. It's true. Every night when I got home there'd be a blackened saucepan on the stove. You see, Shirley, my wife, was doing Continuity on a picture at Beaconsfield at the time. It was close to home, and she left for work after me.'

She frowned, bewildered, but then fastened on to the one word she understood. 'Continuity? She was a Continuity Girl?'

'Yes. And a good one. She was in work all the time.'

'But didn't that mean she was away on location a lot? Didn't you mind that?'

'It wasn't what I minded,' Martin said. 'I mean, she was capable of making these great big gestures, you see. I could get back from the studio and find her gone suddenly, signed up on some picture thousands of miles away. There was even one in Australia, and how much farther can you get than that?'

Lela was still frowning.

'That was quite funny, the Australian picture.' Martin sipped his drink. 'It was an epic, went on shooting for months. And Shirley, well, she was able to stand it for the first month, but then she was ringing up every night, wouldn't you know, trying to get back home. She tried every damn thing she knew to get off that picture, and she managed it in the end. They had to let her go.'

He smiled, remembering. 'They were shooting out in the desert,' he said. 'And the day came when the big man from The Coast, the Studio Head, was flying out to have a look at them. So Shirley, she managed to fix it so that she was the one who met him at the airport.'

His smile broadened. 'What she did,' he said, 'was go off to a car-breaker's yard and find herself a wreck. And I do mean a wreck. It was all squashed up, two feet narrower than it should have been. Its wings were gone, its doors were gone, and all its windows. But the engine was still working, and Shirley paid a lot of money to get the wheels working too.'

He leaned forward. 'So the Studio Head flew in to the airport. And of course there was this line of chauffeurs and limos waiting for the first-class passengers. And there, right at the end Shirley in a Nelson costume, cocked hat, black patch, sword, one arm, the lot. She met the Studio Head and took him over to this wrecked car with no doors. She drove him all the way out of the city, one-handed, one-eyed, and never said a word. And then, when . . .'

He stopped suddenly, noticing Lela glancing at her watch for the second time. 'Is it getting late? Do you need to be back in the office?' he asked, a little sharply.

She drove him back to the Ariadne Hotel, but he didn't

go in. Instead he crossed the road and went in through the gates of the Zappion Gardens opposite. And on, along a moonlit path between dark bushes.

It was the drink, he told himself. Four, no five, brandies.

The drink that had made him talk on and on about Shirley, and the sort of gestures she made.

And the drink now that made him think of his sort of gesture too. The Annie Staedtler sort of gesture.

He was walking towards the Zappion building. There were roasted-nut stalls by it, their gas-jets clustered together in the darkness. And it made him think of Annie, the first time he'd seen her.

She'd been standing on the edge of the set. She had a long walk in to her first shot, and the camera and lights were far away. And there was trouble over there too, the lighting cameraman arguing over the Sinex strips with the director. Big trouble. In the end they decided to re-shoot the whole of the first three days . . . And it was Annie's first picture. She stood there, thin and alone against a single 2-K with a gauze . . . shaking.

Time for the gesture, right? The friendly arm?

Later the Rolls Royces had moved in on Annie Staedtler. Time and again Martin had showed her rushes to fat men. And she got into trouble. She rang Martin every now and then, not often, say once every six months. And he tried to help. But gradually there was very little of Annie left to help. With her breasts hard with silicone, her face soft with alcohol, life became one long operation for Annie Staedtler, under an anaesthetic.

Finally it was her mirror that let her down, the mirror that had got her to where she was. Because the Drug Squad took it away for analysis and found cocaine . . . The fat men dropped her then. And a few months later she died the sort of death the newspapers went to town on.

No, sometimes there wasn't much that was funny about the old days. And sometimes too, not much that was funny about Shirley or himself. The gestures.

It had been there tonight on Lela's face, as she'd turned and looked at her watch. And he'd seen it before on other faces, other Production Secretaries.

Because most of the offices were small nowadays, just offices. And the girls in them just girls, who wore jeans, no make-up, and who drank coffee from cardboard cups.

And whereas he'd always thought there'd been a style about the old days. The eyes of the girls told him he was wrong. Told him that pictures were just pictures, that the Industry he'd known was just an excuse for people like Shirley and him, ordinary people trying to be extraordinary ... And maybe they saw through him too. Sometimes he had an uneasy feeling about it. That what they saw was some fake celluloid Gauguin who'd painted forty years in the South Seas, and now longed to throw it all up and become a bank clerk.

And, he told himself, there could be some truth in that.

A sense of loss came over him as he went back into the hotel, of people who should have been around him and were missing. Even details conspired in this. The face of the man behind the desk was unfamiliar, and of the man who pressed the button of the lift.

In fact there was only one face he knew. It was on the front page of an English language newspaper displayed by the lift, the *Athens News*. A black African face – Dr Aloysius Grivela, the Prime Minister he'd seen on television last night.

GRIVELA DEATH THREAT, the headline said. Second Warning Sent To Athens Conference.

6

He was woken at nine-thirty the next morning by the phone. It was Lela.

'Mr Elegesis is back,' she said.

'Who?'

'Mr Elegesis. Our producer.'

'Oh.' He clutched his head, thinking back. Five brandies? *Five?*

'Listen,' she said, 'the news is good. You remember what Mavromatis was talking about yesterday at the villa? About Jake Mallows trying to hold out for more money, screw up the whole deal, drag it past a certain date?'

'Yes,' Martin said. He didn't.

'Well, he hasn't managed it. Mr Elegesis has won. It took him ten minutes in a courtroom in LA. And now he's back here. The production's going ahead.'

'That's good.'

'It's more than good. Mr Elegesis wants to see you. He wants you here at the office at half-past one.'

'In the middle of the day?' Martin frowned. 'Doesn't everyone sleep then?'

'He's sleeping now,' Lela said. 'He flew in early this morning.'

'And half-past one? Does that mean lunch?'

'No, he's sorry, he's got too many meetings lined up. There are too many people to see.'

'No lunch? What the hell sort of production is this?'

'Listen.' She sounded irritated. 'I've been up half the night. There's an awful lot happening here . . . Oh, and another thing. How many scripts have you read?'

'I don't know. Two. The first two.'

'Well, you'll have to do better than that, won't you? He'll expect you to have read the first six, the first six at least.'

'I suppose so.'

'Okay. Set to work. A car will call for you at one-fifteen. One-fifteen . . . Bye.'

Martin ordered coffee, black coffee. Then he walked over to the marble-topped table where the scripts were. He turned past the first two and looked at the third. And he sighed.

'THE STRIKER'   Episode 3.

FADE IN TO:

1   *THE ACROPOLIS. ATHENS. EXT. DAY.*

The thick fluted pillars, old as time itself, stand tall against a cloudless sky.

2   *A CORNER OF THE PARTHENON. EXT. DAY.*

Two young hippies, CARL and JIMBO, sprawl on the stone steps. They're dressed in tee-shirts and faded jeans. They have the long hair and shrewd questioning faces that upset parents the world over. And they have that itch, that free-booting quality of their kind . . . the modern cowboys.

CARL, carving his name in the stone step with a bowie knife, looks up at the pillars above him.

CARL.

Man, but they do some crazy things in fibre-glass, don't they?

JIMBO.

(two words)

Shi–it.

At one-fifteen the chauffeur called at the hotel. And by one-thirty Martin was following him through the deserted corridors of Antonadis 14. They came to the open door of the Production Office and went in. The room was dim, cavernous, even larger than Martin remembered. The shutters of the tall windows were closed against the afternoon sun. There were scripts and schedules scattered everywhere, and a thick fog of cigarette smoke as though a crowd of people had just moved on.

Only Lela sat there, behind her desk.

Martin went towards her. 'You did say here, didn't you? Here?'

'Yes.' She looked up.

'So where is everybody?'

'Meetings,' she said. 'Meetings all the time. Mr Elegesis is back in his office, as of twenty minutes ago.'

'And he wants me there?'

'Yes. He'll ring when he's ready.' Her voice was strained. He noticed the thin lines around her mouth. But then he remembered she'd been up half the night.

'Dan Leater's with him, too,' she said then.

'Dan.' Martin grinned. 'Dan, my God.'

'Yes, there's something here about him.' She rummaged through the papers on her desk. 'I thought you'd like to see it.'

She found a magazine and gave it to him. It was an American glossy called *Screen Time*. He turned the pages and suddenly found Dan Leater's face staring up at him.

But then he frowned. 'This picture's years old,' he said. 'It was taken way back, when we were working on *Banshee*.'

'Yes,' she said. 'Yes, I suppose it is. He's fatter now, and losing his hair.'

'Vain old sod.' Martin looked on to the headline. 'THE STRIKER – A New Concept In Televisual Entertainment,' he read. My backside, he thought.

He sat down and read on: a challenge, Dan called those godawful scripts, a return to basic story-telling. In Dan's opinion, the filmed TV series was the one area of modern drama that had yet to fulfil its true potential . . . Dan's and his backsides, both.

The phone rang. Lela picked it up. She said a few short

words in Greek, then put it down again. 'Mr Elegesis is ready for you,' she said.

Martin got up and moved towards the door. Then he found the chauffeur blocking his path.

'Is necessity to leave that here.'

'What?'

'That.' The man pointed to the magazine.

'But, I haven't finished.'

'Is necessity. Is for here, for office.'

'Oh, come on.'

'No.'

And suddenly Martin was aware of two things. The tension there was on the man's dark face, and the silence that hung over this office and the next.

He turned to Lela. 'Look, call your doggy off, will . . .?'

The magazine was snatched out of his hands.

'What the hell?'

But Lela got up from behind her desk. 'Don't upset him,' she said. 'He's worked for Mr Elegesis a long time. He's very fond of him, wants everything to be just right. Don't make a scene.'

Outside the office, the silence seemed to stretch through the whole building. They went along the corridor and down the wide marble staircase. There wasn't a sound, not a voice, nor the rattle of a distant coffee cup. They crossed the entrance hall, and as they went outside, a pebble caught under the door. It yelped against the stone step, and the sound seemed to carry right round the courtyard. Nothing stirred there. The sun beat down on the grey cobblestones and the rows of shuttered windows.

The chauffeur sat Martin inside the company Mercedes. Then he drove out under the shadow of the high curving arch. The city beyond seemed very white. The streets white, and the sun white in a white sky. What shadows there were seemed thin and spidery. And to Martin it seemed like an old faded postcard of a city he didn't know.

He looked at the chauffeur then and saw how he kept

glancing at his watch. He saw too how the man was sweating in spite of the car's air-conditioning. The tiny beads that pricked out on the back of his neck, and the way his hands kept slipping on the wheel.

They stopped for a traffic light, turned, and started driving uphill. They climbed through a new business section, passing rows of modern office buildings. Then they turned again and went along a street that traversed the slope. Finally the chauffeur slowed, drew in.

'Is down there.' He nodded. 'Is one black building.'

Martin saw the black marble block down at the end of a short steep street, no more than a hundred yards away.

'Is no possible to go down there.' The chauffeur pointed to the No Entry sign. 'And is maybe too long to drive the other way. You are late maybe for Mr Elegesis.'

'All right,' Martin said, 'I'll walk.' He started to open the car door.

But the man stopped him. 'Is the siesta now. Is everyone asleeping. The *theeroros* is asleeping too, the man who open the door . . . Here.' He held out a key. 'Is for the front door. You go in. You go up to the third floor. Office 354. The office of Mr Elegesis.'

Martin took the key. It had a label which gave the building's address. BOUDAPESTI 3.

7

He got out of the car, and the silence was there again, huge now, hanging over the whole street. Almost eerie . . . Almost nothing, he told himself. It was the siesta, he was in a business section, and every window he could see was shuttered.

He walked away, keeping to the cool of the shade. It went down the street in an even line, ending at the bottom where a broad avenue came across. There was grass down there on the far side of the avenue, and trees that seemed white under the sun's glare.

Halfway down the street, he heard the sound of the car starting up. He turned and watched it drive away. Then he walked on. The buildings were dazzling on one side of him, dark on the other. And at the bottom the black marble of Boudapesti 3.

He reached it, went up the steps, and used the key. The glass door swung the day back at him as he pulled it open. Then he was through to coolness and the smell of new marble. His heels clicked over a white floor as he made his way to the lift. He pressed the button but nothing happened. It was out of order, he decided, and he turned to the stairs.

He was slowing, breathing heavily, by the time he reached the third floor. It was a long passage of new brown parquet. On one side were windows with lowered blinds, thin metal blinds that cast a strange pale light. And on the other side a long row of open doors. He started past them, smelling the smell of new woodstain, new carpets and furniture. Everything seemed new. He walked on past door after door until he came to one labelled 354.

Inside there was a long office, three desks with bright red telephones on them. The blinds were lowered again, and it was dim. Except for a bright square of sunlight at the far end of the room where both a blind and a window were open. Martin turned round and saw an inner door. It was shut, and there was a small frame with sliding panels by its side. One of the panels was drawn back, showing the words *ΔΙΑΣΚΕΨΙΣ* /KONFERENZ.

Conference. Dan Leater was in there with Elegesis. Dan. Martin remembered the last time they'd been together. Three years ago, that picture, that cheapie thriller. And the young earnest producer who'd wanted everything. Everything. Martin smiled. He remembered when they'd been in the dubbing theatre. Reel 9, and a certain shot that had come up, on the screen. A shot of a villain dropping a small washleather bag of diamonds. And the producer had said he'd wanted a track laid over it. The sound of a bag of diamonds falling through the air, he'd said, a thin tenuous sound . . . Dan had hit him over the head with a chair.

Thin tenuous sound.

Suddenly Martin realised . . . that silence again. There wasn't a sound coming from the entire building. Not a voice coming through the closed door. He went towards it, opened it.

There was a small office inside, empty.

He turned back to the room where he stood. He saw the desks again, brand new. The bright red telephones, brand new. Not a paper or a carbon anywhere. Not a cigarette-stub in an ashtray.

And the silence. No hum of air-conditioning. No cool air coming through the vents. He walked quickly over to the light-switches and pressed them. Nothing happened. He was in a new building, brand-new. One that had never been used.

Gradually he turned towards the square of bright sunlight. The window that was open, and the blind. He started walking towards it.

When he was halfway there he heard a sound, a car passing outside. It was on the avenue he'd seen, and it was

45

slowing for the crossroads. Then there were other sounds. Backfires. The squeal of brakes.

He reached the window and looked out. And the first thing he saw, lying on a ledge just below the sill, was something that took him way back. To Bisley, the summers just after he'd left school. A long rifle, a Match Rifle built onto the old P14 action, the sort of rifle he'd used then.

And the second thing he saw took him back too, but not so far. A newsreel shot of 1963.

As if in a dream he looked down at the avenue that was white in the sun's glare, at the grass, the small trees. At the motorcycle cops and the two long black American cars, the first with its rear window shattered. Two men jumped out. The fronts of their suits were messy, there was matter sticking to them. They had pistols. And for a moment they stood alone as the car sped away. Then more men came from the second car. Slim men, in slim suits, with pistols. One of them pointed. At the only window that wasn't shuttered. Then they braced themselves and began firing. At him.

At Martin.

8

For a moment he didn't move. For a moment he looked down at the Match Rifle just below him. It wasn't the one, he knew that. The assassin's bullets would have come from another building, a roof farther along the avenue.

But there was something else he knew.

1963 again. Dallas. The number of shots, the angles of fire, the questions that had never been answered.

This Match Rifle would have been fired. Recently, in the last few hours.

And that was enough. More than enough.

He turned then and went back through the office. He reached the corridor and started walking away. Then he heard the motorcycle sirens outside, three, no, four of them, and he started to run.

At the stairwell, the only thought he had was that in films villains always ran up to the roof. He ran down.

There were three floors, six flights of steps, each flight identical. And gradually they built up a rhythm that hynotised him. Until he *was* in a film.

A film too when he reached the ground floor lobby and heard the pistol butts smashing against the glass doors. He kept to the stairwell and went on down to the basement. There was a store-room he found, with a window on its far side, and he opened it. But then he ducked back. Above him in the sunlight boots were crashing past on the pavement.

He crossed the passage again, came to a store-room on the other side of the building, another window. But he didn't even open it. Because there were strange sounds, sirens again, but shrieking metal Dr Who sirens this time, soft at first, then getting louder. He saw the grey riot coaches pull up. He saw their barred windows, their bristling aerials. Then the steel helmets and the automatic rifles.

He returned to the passage and walked slowly to its end. There was a metal door. He went through it and closed it behind him. He was in the power room. There was the motor of the air-conditioning plant, the motor of the winter heating plant, and the oil tank that fed them both. He looked on. There were switchboards, fuses, water stopcocks, a workbench. And high up on one wall a metal service port, padlocked, with ramps leading down from it. There was no other way out, and nowhere to hide.

He stood there for a moment. He had to give himself up. In films villains gave themselves up.

But suddenly it wasn't a film any longer. There was none of that expectedness, that precision of the silver screen. Outside more riot coaches were arriving. Their shrieks rose to a huge baying ring. And the sound built up a sort of madness in the building. Doors banged, boots clashed on stone, there were high, frightened voices. Then the sudden blast of automatic gunfire. They were more scared than he was. He knew he would be killed.

Concentrate.

The problem was simple. A hiding place. Which meant an enclosed area larger than he was, here in this room.

There was only one. The oil tank.

He climbed up onto it. There was an inspection plate that was bolted down. But it was too small, a circle hardly more than two feet across.

Concentrate. There was no point in making an inspection plate too small for a man to get through.

He took off his shoes and left them on the tank. He ran back to the workshop and found an adjustable spanner. There was a length of rubber piping next to it, and he picked that up too.

On top of the tank, the first bolt was stiff. He moved it a little, but could manage no more. He left it. The second bolt came easily, and the third was finger-loose.

48

He was halfway towards removing it, when he jumped. The blast of another automatic rifle being loosed off. But close now, in the next room. Bullets spattering off the other side of the wall. A scream as someone was hit by a stray. Then silence.

Martin got the third bolt free. He wouldn't touch the last one till then. If it wasn't finger-loose, he was dead.

It was. He worked on it two-handed, the bolt never stopping. It came out. He opened the plate, pivoting it on the first bolt. The stench of oil made him gag. He put one end of the rubber tube in his mouth. He picked up the three bolts and put them in his pocket. He picked up his shoes and the spanner, and lowered his legs into the hole.

The screams were still coming from the next room. Then there were shouts, boots approaching. A sudden storm building up on the other side of the door. A shoulder banged against it.

Martin pushed himself down into the tank. He stopped, caught by his hips.

The door handle turned.

He tore skin from his side. The bolts in his pocket. He was down into foul-smelling darkness as the door opened. Very gently he pulled the inspection plate back into place, leaving a small gap for the rubber tube. And he concentrated on that, just the tube, telling himself he was getting clean air and not the fumes that made his eyes water. There was a vertical rail on one side of the tank, with a float that slid up and down it. He held onto that and kept the oil under his chin.

In the room there were boots, three pairs, going back and forwards quickly. Then they stopped, one after another, and there were voices, words he didn't understand. He knew they were looking round. He knew they were going through the same thought process that he'd gone through. He told himself they were soldiers or policemen. They wouldn't get there.

But they did.

With a small sinking feeling inside him, probably the last one of his life, he took a slow breath, pulled the rubber tube down in his hand, and hauled himself under the oil just as boots crashed against the outside of the tank.

Oil. He forced himself not to think of it as oil. It wasn't oil that was burning his eyelids, his nostrils, creeping up his nose. He almost gagged, almost sucked the stuff up inside him. He screwed his face up tight. From far away he heard the boots, then the other pair, scrabbling on the metal. From far away the inspection plate slide back.

His hands were slipping up the rail, he was coming up. He hooked his foot under something, a filter, something, and pulled himself down. Sounds were hardly there now. Feeling was only there in his hands. He wasn't in oi . . . No, not that word. He wasn't anywhere.

Until the walls of his throat tightened, the cramps began, and his stomach began jerking. He started to panic, knowing he had to fight his way out. Oil. Get air. OIL.

But he was dead if he moved. Death was the blackness that was all round him. The blackness that could reach out and fill every alley he'd ever walked down. He had to hold on. He thought of Shirley. But that was no good. Not the picture he had of her in the last few weeks, the rows. He folded himself very small, and in the tight bands of his stomach, the panic, he found a tiny place. An afternoon, a green afternoon in the garden at home. His daughter Pru, her birthday, and Shirley playing the piano from the house. He held on to that, and it worked.

Boots left the top of the tank, slid down the side. Then the second pair. Martin straightened, felt with his hands, found the rim of the inspection plate, pulled himself up. And then, only then, did he let his breath go, slowly, bubbles bursting at his lips like gunshots.

Then he breathed in. His mouth at the gap between plate and rim. And he held it there.

He held it there for half an hour. While shouts and men moved back and forwards through the building.

After half an hour he pulled himself up until his head was outside the tank and he was leaning on his elbows. There was the thick stench of oil. It oozed from him. His body hung on the lip of the tank like a seal.

He stayed there for two.

Two hours until he heard the boots and men collecting together in the marble lobby. Until he heard their shouts become silence. Heard them march out.

Then there was hammering, the doors being boarded up. Then silence, a long silence that went right through the building.

He got out of the tank, dripping black oil into the metal. He slipped and fell heavily onto the floor. He vomited. Then he passed out.

He came to and found it was 5.30 p.m. He saw the vomit and the oil that spread out from him like a map.

He got up. He left oil everywhere he moved, on everything he touched. He found a tap and drank water. He sat down. Then he drank again. He spent half an hour like that, sitting and then drinking as much as he could hold down.

He felt stronger finally and he looked at the oilmarks all round him. He stripped off his clothes and wrung them as dry as he could. He found a box full of rags and used them to wipe oil from his body. Then, with more rags and a tin of industrial jelly that was on the workbench, he started cleaning the floor.

He didn't pass out again. Every time he felt the fumes rising in him, he crouched with his body bent. The smell of the industrial jelly was strong and clean, it built up a hard thing inside him as he scrubbed with the rags. He removed every trace of oil from the floor, the tank, the workbench. Something told him it was important. Something told him he had only one weapon. They didn't know he was here.

Suddenly it was after seven. He finished, and went back to where he'd left his clothes.

Then he heard noises from the far-off lobby again. Planks being pulled away from the main entrance, boots on marble.

He got back into the tank.

9

They searched more thoroughly now. There were more of them, and they were in the building for four hours. But it helped. Because he had time. When they reached the power room, he was ready for them. He'd wrapped his shirt tightly round his head, and there was the way too he'd found of tying the rubber tube to the float in the tank, tying it where it didn't show, so that he could breathe under the oil. And when it was time, he pulled himself under and breathed slowly, silently, keeping quite still. He thought only of the faces just above him, peering down onto the surface of the oil.

It was a long time after that, nearly eleven, when he heard them form up again in the distant lobby and march out. Again they boarded up the front door. And again there was silence.

He got out of the tank carefully and felt his way through the darkness to the workbench. There was the torch he'd seen there. He found it, switched it on, and went and stood in the rag-box. He stripped off his clothes and let the oil drip from his body onto the rags. He knew he wasn't thinking very clearly. But he knew too there was still just the one thing that would count in his favour. To leave no traces.

It took him nearly an hour to clean up, to wring his clothes as dry as he could and put them on again, and to wrap clean rags around his shoes. Then he left the power room. The torch was in his hand but he didn't use it. He went down the passage, stopping every so often and listening. There was no sound.

He reached the stairwell and climbed to the lobby. It was deserted. He saw the front door, the planks that were nailed across its broken panes, and he started towards it. Started.

Because then he saw the flashing light outside. Outlining the street, the van in the street, and the grey uniforms.

He edged his way back to the stairwell, to a window on the other side of the building. There was an alley, and another flashing light, more uniforms. For a long time Martin looked at them. He saw how there was no cover in the alley, how the light reached every part of it. There was no way out. And he was tired, desperately tired.

He went up the stairs then to the top of the building, the seventh floor. He walked past a row of open doors until he came to the office at the end. He went in, picked up a corner of the carpet, crawled underneath it. And slept.

He woke suddenly, not knowing where he was. A window with metal blinds was just above his head. Sun was coming through it, casting a strange pale light. And around him there were three desks, each with a bright red telephone on it . . . Red telephones. He remembered.

But what he didn't remember, what he couldn't place now, was the sound, the murmur of voices, coming from outside.

He got up slowly and prised a gap in the blinds. And immediately swung back. There were people out there, in Boudapesti Street.

He looked again, carefully. And he saw businessmen and secretaries, staring up towards him, their hands shading their eyes. He saw the pressmen with Nikons, the newsreel teams with Arriflexes.

On the other side of the building, in the alley, the same thing. He was worried then, and started looking for police. But there were no more than six of them, the same number as last night. And they had their backs to the building, were keeping the crowd away.

He watched for some time and came to the conclusion it was just a bloodsucker crowd, wanting to see where it had happened.

Which meant that they thought he'd left the building, got away.

But it also meant he couldn't get away now.

He backed away from the window and blinds, and stood in the centre of the passage. To his left were offices, empty, like the one where he'd spent last night. But to his right, at the passage end, was a plain white painted door. A store room, he found as he went in. And it was there that he had the stroke of luck.

Beyond paint-pots and brushes, trestles and ladders, he found a drawer. It was locked, but he broke it open with a screwdriver. And inside he found half a stale loaf and some chocolate, and a small transistor radio.

He switched the radio on, and after a while found dance music, American dance music.

Then:

'This is the Voice Of America, Rhodes. We interrupt this programme to bring you the latest bulletin on the assassination of Dr Aloysius Grivela, President of Kanawe.'

Grivela. The man he'd seen on television.

'As reported in our last bulletin, responsibility for the assassination has been claimed by the White Settlers, a group of Britishers whose businesses were nationalised when the new state of Kanawe came into being last year.'

The threats Grivela had talked about.

'And this would tie in with the latest communiqué issued by Athens police chief, Kostas Manoussakis. He claims that the assassin, who escaped through a basement window minutes after...'

The window. That window he'd opened.

'... Was now known to be a Britisher. A former movie technician, Martin Baxter Raikes.'

10

He sat outside the store room, his back to the door. He looked down the length of the top floor passage with the radio on his knees. The bulletins came every twenty minutes, and he heard:

Raikes had been seen by three separate bodyguards at the scene of the slaying. Later they'd identified him from his passport at the Ariadne Hotel.

Because police had been called to the hotel. A chambermaid, turning down Raikes' bed, had found $30,000 in notes. Then in the shower she'd found two automatic pistols and an SLR rifle.

Raikes was no stranger to guns. Years back, at his exclusive British public school, he'd been an outstanding marksman. And later at Bisley he'd been one of the youngest competitors ever to reach the final hundred of the famed Queen's Prize. He'd specialised in long range shooting, using a Match Rifle, the same weapon that had gunned down Premier Grivela.

Raikes had been in Athens two days. He'd stayed in one of the city's richest hotels. He'd paid in advance with large denomination bills. Chauffeur-driven cars had called for him.

And yet Raikes, a technician in Britain's depressed Movie Industry, had been out of work two years.

Life had turned so sour for Raikes that, ten days ago, his wife had left him and his two children.

The children were now with his brother in Twickenham, England. This brother had proved evasive with reporters.

When questioned about the first of Raikes' unemployed years, a period reporters were now calling the Missing Year, he claimed Raikes had travelled Europe in a Volkswagen van. He claimed he'd found work picking grapes, and teaching English in schools in Barcelona . . . But to date no record of Raikes' name had been found in any Barcelona school.

Raikes' political views were unknown. But he *was* known to be a patriot. And, during that Missing Year, links with the White Settler Organisation could not be ruled out.

Then there was the money he'd suddenly started spending so lavishly in Athens . . . The brother claimed Raikes was in Greece to work on a TV series called 'The Striker'. It was to be produced by Elpart Productions, with offices in the centre of Athens. It was to star veteran actor Jake Mallows, and be directed by British director Dan Leater.

No TV series of that name had been registered anywhere in the world. No company called Elpart had offices in Athens. Jake Mallows had been in a California clinic for months, and had long cancelled any existing contracts. Britisher Dan Leater had left the Industry two years ago, and was now teaching Film Technique in Australia.

. . . Martin sat quite still.

He stared down at the top-floor passage at the long row of open doors. At the polished parquet floor and the windows with lowered blinds. It was mid-morning now, the light was brighter, luminous, and strangely metal.

And the bulletins went on:

Mrs Shirley Raikes had been found in a Bristol hotel room, which was registered under a man's name. She had leapt to her husband's defence, had claimed to know all about 'The Striker' TV series. But she couldn't explain why she hadn't returned to look after the children while her husband was away in Athens. And when questioned further, Mrs Raikes became violent and struck a reporter.

The Raikes marriage had been a long history of brick-bats. Neighbours talked of wild scenes, breaking glass, of children running round late at night.

At one time Raikes' name had been linked with Annie Staedtler, British movie star who had died in a sixties drug orgy.

And Raikes, after only one day in Greece, had quickly found his way towards a certain section of Athens society. Because a photo had come into the possession of the Alien Police. A photo showing two girls engaged in an indecent act on a sunlit terrace. While Raikes sat beyond them, watching.

. . . Martin found that he was staring on and on at the row of open doors. Noticing how they stood open at different angles, how their glass panels reflected varying shades of light. Like mirrors.

Mirrors at different angles.

And the bulletins went on:

Technicians who'd worked at Raikes' side in British film studios claimed that he was boisterous, a drinker, unpredictable. Which was bad, apparently.

City men, who'd worked in offices with him all those years ago, claimed that he'd left suddenly, dropped out. Which was bad, apparently.

And – Martin was amazed to hear – at that British public school where he'd passed five happy years, he'd been considered strange, a bad mixer, hadn't been liked.

11

Mirrors.

He stood up, moved along the passage, saw himself in the glass panels of the doors.

But not himself.

A strange grey figure walked towards him. A man with a dirty grey film that covered his hair, his skin, and his clothes, that cracked at the joints of his body as he moved. And he moved strangely too, one hand clutching at his stomach as though in pain.

The grey figure went into the first office. It had three desks, three chairs, three bright red telephones.

And the second office exactly the same, three desks, three chairs, three red telephones. And the third, the fourth, the fifth . . . It was as if he weren't moving. As if the walls and floor of the passage were jerking back on their own strange elastic as he turned to go in through another door.

And the elastic, for some reason, was the murmur of the crowd in the street outside. The voices.

And when, by some jump, some tele-portation, he reached the stairwell at the end of the passage and descended the stairs, it was only to find himself in the same place. Because on the floor below there was the same long row of open doors, the mirrors.

And the first mirror he came to, the first office, he'd thought would be the same as all the others. But it wasn't. Because suddenly it wavered and split apart. Its three desks became six, its chairs six, and six bright red telephones.

And the next office, he didn't understand it now, seemed to crumble and grow dim. Tall pillars grew up with tall curving windows between them. There were chipped marble statues and a marble floor . . . The Production Office, he realised, with its scripts on the table and its cans of film.

And then even stranger than that, a film within a film . . . Because Lela was there suddenly. She came from behind her massive carved desk, and stopped in front of him. But stopped exactly, her feet on chalk-marks that were on the floor. She motioned him to stand on chalk-marks too. And then he understood . . . He saw the mike coming down above their heads on its metal boom, saw the lights, the camera. Saw that the walls of the office were the timber and plaster of a film set. And saw the FX Man sitting beyond at his playback console, cueing in traffic noise, phone bells, typewriter chatter.

But he wasn't meant to see all that, he realised suddenly.

Because Lela's face darkened, she became worried . . . What she was doing at that precise moment was handing him a script from a pile. But now she took it back. Instead she searched until she'd found a second script, one that had a large section of coloured re-write pages. And she began talking about re-writes, saying there would now have to be an extra scene. A scene in the courtyard of a villa, she said. There would be talk there, money-talk that he wouldn't understand. And perhaps it would convince him. But even if it didn't, there'd always be the old standby, the Skin Scene, a couple of girls, a couple of press-stud fasteners . . . And there'd be a stills-photographer too, she said. Stills that would be sent to the Alien Police Department, just in case.

She handed him the script. 'Go on. Read about yourself,' she said.

And he read:

76A   *INT. PRODUCTION OFFICE. DAY.*
LELA stands in front of her desk. She hands a re-written script to RAIKES.
LELA.
Go on. Read about yourself.
He bends over the script page.

76B   (INSERT) PAGE OF SCRIPT. DAY.
Which reads . . .
LELA stands in front of her desk. She hands a
re-written script to RAIKES.
                    LELA.
        Go on. Read about yourself.
He bends over the script page.

There was a moment, just a moment, when he saw
clearly. That there was no script, nothing in his hand. That
he was in an office with three desks and three red telephones. That the reflection in the glass panel of the door
showed a grey figure that was bent double, in pain.

And he knew suddenly what it was, as the waves came
and went, as walls and desks blurred and then resolved
themselves before his eyes.

Oil. The same as the grey film that covered his body and
clothes. Oil fumes inside him. And the emptiness, that rack-
ing emptiness since his time in the oil tank last night.

And just as the moment, the clear moment left him, he
remembered the store room on the floor above. The stale
bread in the drawer there, and the chocolate.

Sunlight on blinds was a metal pool through which he swam.
But thick now, the elastic of voices holding him back. And
the mirrors too, the rows of them, showing not one but
hundreds of grey crawling men.

But he made it. Along the passage, up the white marble
of the stairwell, and on to the door at the end of the
passage above. He found the bread and the chocolate, he
found a metal tray and a cold water tap. And he mixed a
paste, bread, water, and just a sprinkling of chocolate.

Then he ate, slowly, feeling the waves coming stronger at
first, the voices coming stronger from outside. But then,
gradually receding.

The voices had gone now, altogether. And for a while he
was worried, thinking he was imagining the silence. Until he

61

looked out through a blind and saw that the crowds had gone, from Boudapesti Street, and from the alley on the other side. Only the police were there, six of them just as before, standing in the shade.

It was the siesta.

Nearly four o'clock by his watch. Half a day had gone.

He sat down then, his back once again pressed against the store room door. And he began to think, but slowly, one thought at a time.

Because he shied away from the unthinkable . . . how they'd done it. How it could possibly have been worth it to them, in terms of time and money, to produce that grey figure of Martin Raikes for the news bulletins. How they even *knew* they could do it.

One thought at a time.

The first of the bulletins. The chambermaid who'd found $30,000 in notes in his room.

Money. It was always believed. Always. The clincher.

Then the automatic weapons in the shower.

But they'd found nothing else. None of 'The Striker' scripts, nor the letters that had come from Elpart Productions.

Letters. They were in the jacket he'd worn yesterday, back in the hotel room. And now gone. If they could plant money and weapons, they could remove the evidence they didn't want found.

Suddenly he realised how close they'd come to him, how little he had. Because he went through his pockets, all of them . . . And found a handkerchief, keys, loose change, a few stained drachma notes, a street map of Athens also stained, a Pentel, sunglasses.

Not very much.

All right. What to do?

Not go to the police, that much was certain. The bursts of gunfire from the basement yesterday were still with him, the clips loosed off by mistake, the screams.

Where then? British soil? The Embassy? He didn't think

he'd be able to convince anyone there, about the real Martin Raikes. But the more he thought about it, he knew it was his only chance.

So when? When to try and break out?

Six policemen, and hard sunlight outside. It would have to be later, after dark. But a long time after dark, he tried to remember what he knew about Athens office hours . . . Nine in the morning till one. Then something like four in the evening till nine . . . So, call it ten, after ten tonight, when the streets would again be deserted.

12

At ten-thirty a grey van came down through the darkness of Boudapesti Street. It stopped outside the building and sounded its horn. Policemen appeared, three of them, then another three. They got into the van and drove away. They were giving up.

Martin made sure. He went down to the ground floor and looked out, both sides. There was no one.

He went on down to the basement, to the window he'd opened yesterday. Now he opened it again, the same one, and he waited, trying to think as clearly as he could.

From his oilstained map of Athens he'd worked out the route from Boudapesti Street to the Embassy. It wasn't far, not much more than a mile. And the map showed square blocks of buildings, regular streets, for the first part. A continuation of the new business section of the city where he now was. He decided to keep to it, and its emptiness, as long as possible.

The second part was more difficult, a huddle of backstreets around a square where two main roads crossed. And the third part . . . He decided on a stretch of open ground, a park that ran parallel to Vasilissis Sofias, the wide avenue that led out to the Embassy district.

He caught sight of himself in the window. His face was cleaner now, he'd scrubbed as much of the oil from it as he could. But his clothes were still thickly matted with grey. People were going to look at him, take a second look. And if he'd been on every radio bulletin, his picture would have been on TV.

Worse, there was the police operation he'd heard about from the radio. It was big. They'd sealed off Athens and Piraeus, set up roadblocks, made sudden arrests with armed patrol cars. He'd heard them through the afternoon, the sirens howling and fading through the streets.

11 p.m. He climbed out of the window.

The first part was easy. The square marble blocks of the business section were as shuttered and silent as when he'd first seen them. But when he came near to the square where two main roads crossed, he suddenly realised he was leaving Diner's Card territory, and everything he knew, behind.

He was standing in a doorway on a long sloping street. The square he was trying to work his way around was one block away. He could see the smoke of its restaurants, hear the blare of *bouzouki* music. And the back-street, the first in the chain he had to go through, lay to his right.

It was drab. Flat cement buildings rose up on either side of a potholed road. Shopfronts were dark, with metal cages lowered in front of them. Above were the wrought iron bars of balconies, with whispers coming from them. And half-way down the street, the bright broad light of a café.

He started towards it. The light became blue, flickering, the light of television. He drew level with the first window and caught a glimpse of rows of faces, all turned towards a small screen. He drew level with the second window . . .

A shout. A man came from a café doorway, straight at Martin, shouting as he came. A large man, in creased working clothes. Martin walked on. The shouts came again. A hand grabbed him, swung him round.

The face was puzzled, frowning, seeming to know him. The hand moved, poked him in the stomach, hard and angry. Martin backed away. The man came on, poking him again and again. His voice rose, became hoarse.

Martin looked over at the café, the faces still in their rows watching the blue light of the screen. He waited a moment longer. Then he ran.

He ran on and on, following the streets, the pattern he remembered from the map. He made one mistake, found himself suddenly going towards bright lights, and faces that were white and startled as they turned. But he swung away, and finally he was through to darkness, open ground, the park.

There were low bushes, and he sank into their cover. He crouched there for five, ten minutes. But no sound came from behind.

He straightened then and looked around him. He was on high ground. The park was sloping, mainly grassland, but a strange coarse-fibred sort of grass that creaked underfoot as he moved. The bushes stretched on away from him, laid out in ornamental whirls, down towards some sort of memorial. And beyond, at the bottom of the slope, was the wide six-lane avenue that was Vasilissis Sofias. A trolleybus whined slowly down there, stopping at empty stops, ahead of time. It was making its way towards large modern buildings, the Embassy area.

The British Embassy was square and ugly, like a pile of shoeboxes under the stars. Streetlights showed its concrete walls, the rougher concrete of its beams. To one side of it there was a short drive, a no-nonsense affair between stark walls. And at its end, a lit doorway. Two policemen stood there. Were they always there? Martin wondered. If he had to put money on it, he thought they probably were.

And if he had to put money on it too, he thought they'd stop him. He was supposed to have committed a crime on Greek soil. And British soil? It was inside the doorway. But did it extend as far as the lit pavement outside? Would the police risk a struggle, unbutton their holsters, right on the Embassy steps?

All right, a few bruises, a beating maybe. There was no other way.

He left the shadows where he stood, and the two men stiffened, watching him. He walked slowly at first towards the drive, the lit doorway, but then he moved quicker, building up a momentum.

66

Car doors opened behind him.

Four men, with pickhandles, running. Not police. Not with pickhandles. Then who?

He ran towards the doorway. They ran behind him, faster. He was just at the edge of the light when the first pickhandle fell. He went on a few paces, screaming, shouting at the police.

A voice from behind him shouted too, just two calm words.

The policemen turned away, walked away. Both of them.

13

He was lying on the floor in the back of the car. It was large, an old rattling Peugeot, moving quickly. And the shoe, the shoe that had been pressed down onto his face for the past ten minutes, was still there. Then it moved. The sweating man with the rolls of fat, the man who'd hit him four times with the pickhandle beckoned. Martin waited a moment, then pulled himself up.

He was required to kneel behind the driver's seat as the car slowed, then stopped. The sweating man gripped his head and showed him the area of waste ground, the wooden poles there, and the broken breeze blocks. Where it was going to happen.

He showed him how too. With his pickhandle he tapped Martin first on the nose, then on the windpipe, then on the temple. He showed his watch, raised one finger for one minute, then scraped his hands, palms downwards, apart.

No. Not police.

The three in the back were close around him, their breath around him, as the car mounted the pavement. It lurched over the rough ground. Then the driver whistled suddenly and swung the wheel. Martin just had time to see the small fire ahead, and the tramps who were huddling near it for warmth.

They turned back onto the road and drove on. The sweating man showed his watch again, raised two fingers for two minutes. Then he leaned forward to Martin's right, looking out for another place.

Wooden poles, Martin saw them again, but lashed together now to form scaffolding. And behind them breezeblocks, rows of blocks, making grey walls. A building site. They were passing through a building site, the road wet and shining ahead where a hose trailed across it. And they were driving fast.

He was kneeling between the front seats, just an arm's length from the wheel. He leaned forward, grabbed it, swung it. The car skidded, ballooned on its old springs, went over. There was a huge grinding as it slid on its roof. On and on. In slow motion it seemed bodies were falling all round him. He was trapped underneath, pushed towards the door. The car kicked against a curb, rolled again, on its side, its wheels. The door came open. And he helped it. Suicidally he pushed himself out.

He was spinning suddenly, feet, hands, sky spinning around him, and only the pain, the burning pain of the road wherever it touched.

He stopped. The spinning didn't stop, only his body, the ache of it. And he heard the crash as the car smacked, roof down, into a trolleybus post. Overhead the wires lurched, sang. But the post stayed upright. And the car was crumpled, bent crookedly around it. There were screams.

He couldn't move, he felt sick, shaking. He couldn't move even when a figure pulled himself up through the broken glass of a window. The fat man. But he started walking in circles, round and round in circles. There was blood coming from his head. He kept raising his hands then letting them fall again, as though afraid to touch it.

Martin moved. Slowly he got up. His left leg hurt. Pain stabbed at him every time he put weight on it. But he shuffled away, dragging it behind him. He reached the far curb, then the scaffolding and the shadow of the breeze-block wall. And he looked back.

The fat man was kneeling by the car now, trying to pull himself up. By him a wheel was still spinning, rumbling on its axle. And from inside the car the screams were steady and terrible.

Martin leaned against the wall. Carefully he felt his legs, the right and the left, and then his arms. There were no bones broken. The stab of pain still came as he put his left foot to the ground, but he saw the asphalt burns there, and the tatters of his trouser leg. And he realised something else too, the heel of his left shoe had been ripped away, causing him to limp.

He felt his body then, and his head. There was no blood, nothing was broken inside him. He saw the burns again on his side, on his right forearm and hand. But the rest was shock. He stood there awhile until he'd made himself believe that. Then he limped away, leaning his weight on the wall.

At its end there was a wicket fence, and lights. Cobbled streets fanned out away from him between warehouses. He chose one and started down it. By the end of the street he was no longer leaning his weight against the wall. And the pains he felt came only from certain areas, from the bruises and burns he'd noticed before. He was whole . . . More, the pain was sharpening his mind. For the first time he was thinking clearly.

He knew the next step.

14

He got the number from the phone book. He dialled it, put a two-drachma piece in the slot. Then, grunting with pain, he reached up and broke the overhead light in the booth.

The dialling tone was interrupted by a voice, hoarse, snatched from sleep. *'Embros?'*

'Halkis?'

There was silence.

'Halkis?'

A longer silence.

'Halkis? You surprised to hear from me?'

'No. I . . . I was almost expecting it.' The voice was shaky, afraid. 'I was going to get out today, when my wife and kids went. But I had to leave it till tomorrow.'

'Get out?'

'Out of Greece.'

'What?'

'Martin, you don't understand.' Halkis' voice rose. 'That evening when we met, when we talked . . . Don't you see? They would have been watching you. And they would have seen me too, got the number of my car.'

Car? A Rolls Royce? And the man's wealth? The palace he'd talked about? 'Halkis, what the hell have you got to be afraid of?'

'You don't understand,' the man repeated. 'You just don't understand.'

'I understand one thing,' Martin said. 'I mean, you knew, didn't you? What was going to happen to me?'

There was a pause. Then: 'Yes. At the end, right at the end of our talk, when you showed me the letter.'

'And you ran away?'

'Martin, I tried to say something. Believe me, I tried. But . . .'

'But, what?' Sweat stood out on Martin's face. He gripped the phone wire, the only thing that held him to the man. 'Look, Halkis, your wife and kids are out of the country now, you said so. Tomorrow you're leaving too. And I can't stop you . . . So, all right. Put the phone down and finish the job.'

There was a much longer pause. 'What d'you want?' Halkis asked then.

'Food, brandy, clothes, money, information . . . And twenty minutes of your time.'

'Twenty minutes?' Halkis hesitated. 'There'll be no trouble?'

'Trouble? For Christ's sake, every policeman in Athens is looking for me. And then there's the others, Christ knows who they are.'

He waited, still sweating.

'All right,' Halkis said then. 'I'll come. Where are you?'

Martin told him. Then he left the phone booth and went away to the shadows.

He still kept to the shadows as the car drew up. Not the Rolls Royce he'd been expecting, but an old battered Taunus. He waited a moment longer, making sure Halkis was alone, and that there were no new shadows down the street, no police. Then he crossed the pavement and opened the car door.

Halkis looked up, alarmed by his limp, his tattered clothes. *'Panagia mou,'* he said. 'In the back. Get in the back and lie down.'

'The back. I'm getting used to that.'

'What?'

'Nothing.' Martin opened the back door and got in.

Halkis' self-possession, the crisp white of his shirt-front, lasted just as long as it took for the door to close again. Then his hands shook as he engaged gear and started away.

72

'There are roadblocks on all the main roads out,' he said. 'I'm going to drive around near the Centre. And it's twenty minutes. No more.'

Martin nodded. There was a rug on the back seat, and he lifted it. The first thing he saw was a bottle of brandy. He raised it to his mouth, took three, four long pulls, and gasped as the warmth hit him. Then he looked on. There was a shirt, a jacket, and a pair of jeans.

'My wife's jeans.' Halkis was watching him in the mirror. 'She's bigger than I am. I'm sorry, it was the best I could do.'

Martin put them on. They fitted, except that they were inches too short. He put the shirt on, and then the jacket.

'There's 30,000 *drachs* in the pocket, just over £200,' Halkis said. 'There's food there, in a basket . . . And as for information, just remember that anything I tell you, I'll deny later. It never happened.'

'All right,' Martin said. 'Just keep driving. And stay away from the horn.'

He found the basket, the beef, chicken, and bread that were inside it, cold from a fridge. He took another long pull from the brandy bottle and he began to feel human. He leaned forward, larger than Halkis, and the man seemed to grow nervous.

'Okay, for starters, your job with the diplomatic service,' Martin said. 'What is it?'

Halkis told him, and he whistled.

'So, the Greek government,' he said then, 'did it have anything to do with the assassination? The killing?'

'No.'

'But it knew?'

Halkis didn't answer.

'It knew,' Martin said. '*You* knew, didn't you, that first night we met? You told me that much on the phone.'

And slowly Halkis nodded.

'All right then, the people who set this thing up, are they Greeks?'

'No, they're outsiders. And they stayed outside the country all the time.'

'But they used Greeks?'

'Just a few.'

'So who are they? These outsiders?'

Halkis half-turned from the wheel. 'That I don't know,' he said. 'Truly I don't.'

Martin thought for a moment. 'That group of Englishmen,' he said then. 'The White Settlers, or whatever they're called. Is it them?'

'No.'

'But, on the radio .. ?'

'They had a certain amount of publicity.' Halkis nodded. 'And they even claimed responsibility for the killing afterwards.'

'Well, then?'

'The White Settlers.' Halkis shrugged. 'As far as it's possible to tell, they're just a couple of blimpish colonels and a few young sadists, sitting in an office in England. Don't you see? They were used, just as you were used. They're not in this sort of league.'

'What d'you mean?'

'Money,' Halkis said. 'I mean money.' Then he paused. 'Martin, where do I begin? Assassination and counter-assassination, they're an industry nowadays. They're a pile of papers that high on my desk . . . There are certain people, people who appear in the papers every day, who've almost forgotten what sunlight feels like. The US Secretary of State, for example, he flies to certain countries with an armoured car in his plane. And when he steps out of that car, it's behind bullet-proof walls . . . Look, Martin, there are buildings going up today with steel-lined garages, steel-lined lift-shafts. They have apartment-windows which are sited to exclude angles of fire. And they've even got guardsmen, guardsmen drawn in on the architect's plan.'

Martin stared.

'Obviously I'm not talking about the smaller killings,'

Halkis went on, 'where the man waits on the street corner with the automatic weapon, or where the hand-grenade is lobbed through the office door . . . I'm talking about world-leaders, and other leaders too who are rated as extremely politically sensitive from time to time.'

'Like Grivela?'

'Grivela, yes, at the moment.' Halkis shrugged uneasily. 'Martin, it's no exaggeration to say that you could have run Grivela's day-to-day programme through a computer, and come up with no more than six *minutes* in six months when he was . . . accessible.'

'And those six minutes? You're trying to tell me they came here in Greece? At the Athens Conference?'

'No. Or not as far as Grivela's staff thought. I mean, we supplied him with a half-armoured car . . . we don't, as it happens, possess a fully-armoured car in Greece . . . But the routes that car took were carefully selected and cleared.'

'And yet you say you *knew* there was going to be a killing?'

'No. But we had a good idea. Or more than a good idea. Because what we knew was the amount of money a certain organisation was spending here in Greece. It all gets back to money. Don't you see?'

'No.'

'A half-armoured car,' Halkis repeated. 'A car with side windows and bodywork bullet-proofed. Where the only possible shot is through the rear window. And where that car is averaging, *averaging*, 40 mph through deserted siesta streets . . . You still don't see?'

And he didn't.

'Look, Martin, the man who makes that shot . . . who *guarantees* to make that shot . . . well, there aren't going to be many people in the world like that, are there? I mean, he's not going to be the man of the popular thriller, the man who opens a briefcase and screws together a small gun that looks like a drainpipe. Well, is he? . . . You know

75

better than that. You know about rifles, long range rifles, shooting at long range.'

'Yes,' Martin said. 'Yes.' He'd never really thought about it before.

'That man,' Halkis said, 'he gets paid a great deal of money. A million, maybe more. And there are expenses, huge expenses, he's going to insist on those too. Because there's something else he's going to guarantee . . . that he gets away.'

There was a pause. Martin stared at his hands. 'You mean me?' he said then. 'Using me? Setting me up as a fall-guy, just so he can get clear?'

'Yes,' Halkis said. 'But that's only part of it.'

'What's the other part?'

'If you had power, a great deal of power,' Halkis lowered his voice, 'and you wanted a certain political leader killed. While at the same time you wanted no trace of the killing to come back to you . . . How would you go about it?'

'I don't know. How?'

'Well, the best of all possible worlds would be to have that political leader killed,' Halkis said. 'And then, as quickly as possible, have the assassin killed too . . . Or appear to have him killed.'

'What?'

'Think,' Halkis said. 'Think of Dallas.'

'You mean, the same thing there?'

'I don't know. Millions of words have come out of Dallas. American-style words, overkill . . . And why? A rifle that couldn't possibly have fired all the shots it was supposed to? not in the time? Or an assassin, a strangely one-dimensional figure, and yet where every one of the few facts known about him pointed the same way? . . . I told you before, as a method it's text-book.'

He slowed the car and swung the wheel. They turned into a long uphill road where buildings were blue and ghostly under the street-lamps.

'But you mean,' Martin said then, 'you mean they picked

me out, they got me all the way from England, they arranged a string of phoney film-offices, film-scripts, secretaries? Just to help kill one African politician?'

'Yes.'

'But why? Why was Grivela killed?'

'It isn't the killing, not the bullets going through the car window,' Halkis said. 'But what that killing means.'

'And what does it mean?'

The man hesitated, uneasy.

'Come on.'

'Well,' he said. 'It's the timing as much as anything else.'

'The timing?'

'Let's just say that Grivela happened to be in the wrong place, his country Kanawe, at the very wrong time,' Halkis said. 'Look, it can't be any news to you that a lot of changes are going to take place in Africa, very sweeping changes. But what could be news to you is that . . . in certain people's opinion . . . these changes are going to come far more quickly than anyone imagines. Not in three years' time, nor even next year. But next month . . . next week . . .'

'And these people,' Martin said, 'the people who hold these opinions, who are they?'

Halkis didn't answer.

'Friends of Greece?'

'Friends of Greece.' The man nodded. 'That's as far as I'll go.'

'Come on,' Martin said again.

And Halkis was even more uneasy. 'Let me put it another way,' he said. 'If our police force finds out that a certain political killing is due to take place in this country, then we have a simple choice, don't we? Do we let it happen, or not?'

'For Christ's sake, just like some football match?'

'Exactly. You surely can't imagine these things don't happen, in any country of the world, just because you never hear about . . .'

But Martin grabbed his shoulder. He was watching Halkis

closely, the sweat that stood out on his face. 'Come on,' he said. 'There's more.'

And Halkis began to speak quickly, jerkily, as though his mind were trying different avenues. 'Understand. I don't take decisions. I have papers placed on my desk,' he said. 'And, Martin, you must believe me. I admire the English, I always have. And you're my friend.'

'English? What's that about the English?'

'Well, surely you must see, a major political crime, committed in this country, by England, it . . . it could fit in with certain internal developments here.'

'What the hell are you talking about?' Martin was amazed.

'Simply this.' Halkis grew calmer. 'To a large part of the Greek people, the English are seen as being hand-in-glove with the Americans. And of course there was the American support for the *junta* here, a few years back. Not to mention NATO giving half of Cyprus away when the *junta* fell.'

'I don't understand.'

'Martin, that's just it. Go even farther back to thirty years ago. You British helped us win the war. But at the same time you started another one, a civil war here in Greece, that lasted even longer than the original war. And, all right, you were tired. You felt you had to choose one side or the other . . . But, Martin, how many of your countrymen even *know* about it?'

Martin nodded.

'Sometimes,' Halkis said. 'Sometimes Europe gets the impression that the English spend half their lives watching infantile German prisoner of war films on TV, and the other half begging money from the West German Repub—'

Suddenly the car rose over the crest of a hill. Ahead in the street there were lights, cars, a blockade.

'Left. Turn *left*,' Martin shouted.

As Halkis swung the wheel, he threw himself down onto the floor of the car and pulled the rug over him. And there were new thoughts now . . . *Martin, I don't take decisions. I have papers placed on my desk.*

There was a small gap in the rug through which he could see. He knew they were driving down a dark street, heard the sound of sirens starting up from behind.

Then ahead. From a street ahead of them and to their right. Headlights flashing across them.

Halkis braked.

They were locked in by lights now, and the howl of sirens. Boots came running. Hands, rifles, banged against the car.

Through the gap Martin saw the man in the steel helmet, the carbine hanging down from his shoulder. He was shouting, wrenching at the car door.

Then, as he got it open, Halkis was shouting too. But shrilly, with a schoolmaster's anger. He pushed the man's hands away . . . And from his pocket produced a small identity folder.

The man took it, read it, and immediately backed away. He clicked his heels, waved the others away too, and muttered apologies, on and on.

Halkis sat there as men, lights, sirens, disappeared. He waited until the street became dark again and then he drove on.

'Thanks,' Martin said. 'Thanks.'

But Halkis was afraid, his hands shaking on the steering wheel. And he passed no more than three side streets before he suddenly turned and parked in a row of cars.

'Right,' he said. 'That's the end. You get out. I get out. I take the first plane out of the country, and we never see each other again.'

'What?'

'Nothing. I'm leaving the car here.'

'The car?'

'Yes.'

'What is it about the car?'

Halkis didn't answer.

'What?' Martin reached out for him.

'I've never been stopped driving it before,' Halkis said strangely. 'Never, ever.'

Martin looked round then, at the battered interior of the old Taunus, and on to Halkis' expensive clothes. There was something he didn't understand.

'I mean it,' Halkis said. 'We both leave now.'

'No.' Martin's grip tightened. 'Twenty minutes. You said twenty minutes, remember? And that's what it's going to be.' He turned away, frowning, trying to forget the car and Halkis' strangeness about it . . . trying to get his mind back to before the police blockade.

'All right,' he said finally. 'The Greek political scene. Take it that I help somehow if I get gunned down on some Athens street corner . . . I don't understand it. But now I want facts. Hard facts.'

'Like what?'

'Like that first evening we met in the café. The letter I showed you. What was it about the letter?'

Halkis hesitated. Martin pulled his face close.

'The signature down at the bottom,' Halkis said then. 'Lela Kalastiria.'

'Lela?'

'Yes.'

'Who is she?'

'Well, the police, the military police they've had her on a list for some time.'

'Just that?'

'No. They knew where she lived, where she was picking up her messages, and they intercepted them. They did what's known as a plumber's job, and it was then they found out about the assassination . . . about an Englishman who . . .' He turned suddenly. '. . . Martin, I swear to God I didn't know it was you. Not until I had your Film Company letter in my hand.'

Martin watched him. Then he nodded. 'All right. Let's stick with Lela. You say you know where she lives?'

'Lived. She's gone underground now. Like the rest of them, I imagine.'

'But you said something about messages?'

'Yes,' Halkis said. 'That's still the same. She still picks them up in the same place.'

'Where?'

'A café. Out in a suburb called Harokopou.'

'And when does she pick them up?'

'Every day. She goes every day.'

'What time?'

'It's never the same time. The café's open from eight in the morning till midnight.'

'What's the name of this café?'

'Kristakis'.'

'Write it down,' Martin said, 'in English and in Greek.'

Halkis did so, with a small silver pencil on a pad.

'Now show me where Harokopou is on the street-map.'

Halkis took the crumpled oilstained paper, and ringed a cross-roads, far out on one corner.

'Now,' Martin said, 'is there anything else you know about this Lela?'

'She's a hard woman,' Halkis said. 'She's worked for one liberation organisation or another since she was fourteen. She comes from Cyprus.'

'Any boyfriends?'

'None we know about.'

'And what about contacts? You said you intercepted messages? Did a plumber's job?'

'We didn't go any farther after that,' Halkis said. 'It was when we decided to leave it alone, let the thing happen. We . . .'

He broke off suddenly, looked at his watch. 'Martin, that's all I know. Truly. You have to let me go now. I have to get out of this car.'

His voice was high, his hand was scrabbling towards the doorhandle. His fear had returned.

That strange fear Martin was sure had nothing to do with the assassination, or the police manhunt.

But the car. It was to do with the car.

Once again Martin looked at the scarred dashboard, the worn seats. Then on to Halkis, his gold watch, cufflinks, silk shirt.

And then, just for a moment, he caught a glimpse of something on Halkis' face. Something, he didn't know quite why, that took him back, years back . . .

To school.

'Halkis,' Martin said then. 'You know, when I was waiting for you just now, outside that phone booth, I only half-expected you to turn up.'

Halkis didn't look at him.

'There you were,' Martin went on. 'Your wife and kids out of the country. You yourself getting out within hours. So why not leave it? Why not run out on me a second time?' He paused. 'I mean, it wasn't anything you felt you owed me . . . Or was it?'

Still Halkis didn't look at him.

'The only answer I could come up with,' Martin said, 'was a day a long time ago, at school. A grey afternoon. You sitting alone in a classroom, while everyone else was outside. And you were alone because you were in trouble.'

Halkis slumped down in the driving seat. Martin watched him. And he didn't put it into words, those long-ago words of school. The young kids, fresh from prep school, who'd been called Tarts. The Top Twenty of Tarts. The sweets, the favours, the meetings in the end squash-court . . . Words that Martin hadn't had any truck with. But only because the loneliness, the isolation of the school hadn't affected him in that way. Like a few others he'd pored over the pages of *Health & Efficiency* magazine . . . Health and farting Efficiency. He almost smiled.

But he didn't. Because Halkis' trouble had been serious that afternoon. There'd been a certain Levantine seriousness of his, tricks he had . . . and money. Halkis was being black-mailed by two other boys for fifty pounds.

And Martin had given help, a Bulldog Drummond sort of help, bruised a few mouths. He didn't know quite why. Except that maybe, as boring old Bulldog would have said, blackmail was an ugly word.

He looked at Halkis now. 'This car, this cheap beat-up old car,' he said. 'The car you've never been stopped while driving. Never ever . . . Let's put that against your high-powered diplomatic job.'

Halkis turned away.

'You use it to drive somewhere, don't you? You've got a place? A place here in Athens nobody knows about?'

Slowly the man nodded.

'Nobody? Nobody at all?'

'No.'

'And is there anyone there? Staying there?'

'No.'

'You're sure?'

'They're just casuals.' The words were almost inaudible.

'What's the address?'

'*Athinai tria-cossa-pende.*'

'Write it down, in English and in Greek. Then give me the key.'

Halkis got out his silver pencil and pad again. He wrote. Then he turned to the ashtray above the car-radio. He pulled it out. And in the cavity behind were three keys, and a small cardboard booklet.

'What's that?' Martin asked.

'Driving licence.'

'Greek?'

'Yes.'

'In your name?'

'No. In the name of Dimitri Pavlos.'

'Who's he?'

'He doesn't exist.'

83

'Hand it over,' Martin said. 'And then you can drop me off at this place of yours.'

Halkis drove, stiff and pale behind the wheel. It took ten minutes. Then he stopped, let Martin out, and drove away. And he never once looked at Martin, or spoke.

15

And once he'd used the keys, Martin found out why. Because Halkis had a very unusual apartment, or rather two apartments, connected by a locked door. Each was separate, and each had its own front entrance. One in Athinai Street, where Halkis dropped him, and one in the street running parallel.

Athinai Street was wide and potholed, a broad grey ribbon under the stars, leading straight towards the distant square cliffs of the Acropolis. To Martin's right the roofs were long and shadowy, drumming with a metallic sound in the wind. Market roofs, he found as he got nearer, the hall of a large permanent market.

The entrance to *tria-cossa-pende*, 305, lay at the end of an alley. There were rows of market stalls on either side, metal and shuttered. Martin could see the crowds that would be here in daytime, could see Halkis passing unnoticed among them. And the door he unlocked was small and inconspicuous.

Inside there was a steep flight of stairs, whitewashed, with only the half-moons of their treads left to darker stone. And white too was the colour of the three rooms at the top. Small rooms, bare, almost cell-like. There was a bathroom that was primitive and Greek. A kitchen with an old stone sink, a curtained alcove, and two straw-seated chairs. And in the bedroom just a bed, coat-hangers on a wire, and a barred window. Through it he could see the Acropolis, but from higher up now, the columns of the Parthenon pale in the moonlight.

With the other keys in his hand, Martin unlocked the door to the second apartment. And immediately the cell-like atmosphere was gone. Immediately he could see the need for it. The two sides of Halkis were there in front of him.

The smell of leather hit him as he opened the door. It was everywhere, lining the walls, the floor, and the ceiling, flaring in the light of the lamps. The furniture was leather too, massive and buckled. There were rows of bottles, drawers of pills, and shelf after shelf of books.

The books were of photographs of men. There was a strange chill to them, an otherness, an impenetrable world. Because there were devices too, a great many that Martin couldn't guess the meaning of. Nor could he guess what led up to them, what came after them, or where the progress was that lay at the centre of human undertaking. That was the shock, and the sameness of the photographs too, the obsessions endlessly repeated with just a slight change of angle. It was impossible to tell why, which was better than the others. There was just the quality of them, the minutely reproduced detail.

He left the books, moved on, and came to another leather-lined room. But this one was strange. It was like a hollow pyramid on its side. Walls, floor, and ceiling narrowed to a point. And in that point there was something that looked like the horn of an old-fashioned gramophone, leather too, some vast black lily. Martin looked at it. He turned away but found no other room. Then he came back and looked at it again. And he saw that in the centre of the lily there was a hole, large enough for a man to get through.

His feet slipping on the shiny sloping floor, Martin reached the entrance and went in.

He stayed only a moment. The devices were there, the ones in the photographs. But the room . . . if you could call it that, dome-shaped, with a soft floor into which he sank up to his waist, with tunnels, labyrinths . . . the room was like standing inside some vast black brain.

He didn't breathe out until he'd returned to the first apartment, the white cell-like bedroom. He looked at the bare walls, just as Halkis must have done, countless times.

He looked through the window at the Parthenon, and he sat down on the bed. He put the memory of that locked door, and what lay behind it, out of his mind. And he thought.

A small white room in the centre of Athens, he thought. And nobody knew about it, except for Halkis. And he wasn't going to say anything, that much was certain.

A girl, Lela Kalastiria, turning up at a café in a place called Harokopou, he thought, sometime between eight in the morning and midnight.

But getting her back here.

How?

A hard woman, Halkis had said. A member of one liberation organisation or another since the age of fourteen.

He looked around him then, at the bare whitewashed rooms. He couldn't go back behind that locked door.

In the bedroom there was nothing, just the bed and the coat-hangers on the wire.

In the kitchen, behind the curtain of the alcove, there was a small camping-gas stove. There were Greek coffee cups, glasses, utensils, and tinned food.

In the bathroom there were toothpaste and soap . . . and an old-fashioned razor. Halkis used a cut-throat.

Twice Martin left the razor and went away.

Then he came back a third time. He took the razor out to the flight of stone stairs, and ground it back and forwards on the topmost step. On and on.

Until it was as blunt as a butter knife.

16

It was 7 a.m. when he left by the door to the market. It was already crowded, a meat market, he realised. Maybe Halkis had a sense of humour. The stall-holders certainly had . . . Passing close to a display of fresh red meat, Martin noticed the lamps that shone down onto it. Each with a strip of red cellophane taped over its bulb.

Outside Athinai Street was grey, the light all in the sky, waiting. He walked through crowds, and past doorways with racks of war-surplus clothing hanging inside. And he went shopping. He bought shoes, a creased khaki cap, an ex-US windbreaker, and he threw Halkis' expensive jacket away. Then at a kiosk he bought new sunglasses and a Greek paper. He looked at himself in the kiosk window. The oil, from that basement tank in Boudapesti 3, was helping him now. His hair was matted and grey. His face was somehow longer, exhausted, with dark lines still clinging to the creases. Maybe he'd get by. And there was his trump card too, the Greek driving licence under the name of Dimitri Pavlos.

He went down to the end of Athinai Street, where his map told him there was a Metro station. He found it in a square where motorcycle vans racketed past in the dust of potholes. Like all Greek squares it seemed to be crumbling apart at the edges. And that was exactly how Martin felt. He hadn't slept, there was a buzzing in his ears. And, as he joined the queue of workmen at the ticket window, he didn't think he cared any more about policemen.

Which was what got him through. Because the train stopped for some time at a station called Petralona, and two policemen got into the carriage. But it was crowded with workmen who gradually became angry. And Martin,

88

when his turn came, showed the driving licence without looking up. The policemen passed on.

He reached Harokopou at ten minutes to eight, and he saw the café called Kristakis'. It stood on a corner of the cross-roads Halkis had marked, between the main road and a backstreet. It was one of that new, slightly desolate, kind of cafés. A wide bleak interior, rows of yellow plastic chairs and tables standing on a fake marble floor. And fronting the whole, a broad-meshed metal grille. It wasn't yet open.

Martin turned. He looked across the backstreet to a small ornamental garden on the far side. It had low wispy trees with benches in their shade. And the farthest bench, set close among the trees, was hidden from all sides except the café. He went over there, sat down, and opened the newspaper.

At eight the shutters of the café slid up. A man in an apron came out and started lowering a yellow awning. Then he arranged the yellow plastic chairs and tables in its shade. Finally he switched on an orange drink cooler. The liquid in its glass bowl was yellow too, bubbling, with plastic oranges dancing on its surface.

He heard the sound of cars passing on the main road, coming from the grey metallic haze that was Piraeus and going on to the grey metallic haze of Athens. Cars, and the occasional whine of a trolleybus. Then their noise slackened, the rush hour came to an end. The sun climbed higher, the shade shifted, and Martin shifted with it. He could see farther down the side street now, the building that was next to the café. A battered cement building, with pencil marks and scratches round its doorway. There was a blue sign

ΦΡΟΝΤΙΣΤΗΡΙΑ ΤΗΣ ΑΓΓΛΙΚΗΣ ΓΛΟΣΣΗΣ
ENGLISH CLASSES.

And on the door itself was a crude child-drawn poster. GRAND SUMMER CONCERT, it said, BALLETO.

A bell sounded. Children streamed out of the doorway

and across to the ornamental garden. Martin was worried that they'd come right up to where he sat, ask him questions, perhaps talk later about the foreigner they'd met. But they played, a hissing game, one with his back turned to the others, like Grandmother's Footsteps.

Then there was a second bell. The children went back into the school. He could see some of them through a window. They were high up, on some sort of stage at the end of a classroom. They were rehearsing, for the Grand Summer Concert, he imagined. And a woman teacher kept shouting, 'No ... No ... *No.*'

The main road was almost silent now. There was just the stutter of local traffic, motorcycle trucks, scooters, and the occasional whine of a trolleybus. It was almost eleven. The sun was overhead, and the shade had long since left Martin. The tiredness came back, and the buzzing in his ears. He began to be obsessed by the orange drink cooler, the bubbling yellow liquid, but he knew he shouldn't leave his hiding place among the trees.

Then, incredibly, he heard the sound of the Charleston. At first he didn't believe it, thought he must be dreaming. But it was real, an old scratchy gramophone record coming from the school . . . And then he saw them, four young girls up on the stage in the classroom, rehearsing again, but this time for the Balleto.

They were a chorus line, in flapper costumes they'd made themselves out of crêpe paper. They wore cloche hats, shift dresses with short Twenties skirts, and ribbons of paper that wound criss-cross up their legs. But they were solid Greek girls, they danced solidly, and the ribbons kept unwinding. 'No,' the woman teacher kept shouting. 'No . . . *No.*'

He almost missed Lela. There was the whine of a trolleybus, rising as it drew away from a stop. And then a woman appearing past the end of the low trees. She had her back turned, was walking away. And gone was the shining blonde hair, the fashionable European clothes. Only from the way she walked was she Lela.

She stopped on the corner, waiting to cross. And he had a choice. He could take her now, or later when she came back from the café. But by then she would be facing him.

Six quick paces took him to her. Four quick paces brought her back to the shade of the trees. Then he let his windbreaker fall open, let her see the razor.

He took it out, moved the blunt blade nearer and nearer, then rested it against her cheek.

'You've only got to say one word,' he said, 'and it happens.'

She didn't move.

'There's a taxi rank just up the street,' he said then. 'We're going over there. Slowly.'

He got her into the taxi, holding her close, his other hand keeping the razor just inside his jacket. And he sat very close to her on the back seat.

'*Athinai tria-cossa-pende,*' he said to the driver.

17

She walked ahead of him up the whitewashed stairs, placing her feet exactly in the half-moons of bare stone. He pushed her on into the small kitchen.

And it was there for the first time that he saw her. Not just the absence of European clothes, of blonde hair, but saw her as she was.

A hard woman, Halkis had said.

And she was, but in some dark immovable way. She stood firmly, bare-legged in flat heels. There was the strong square line of her shoulders, the rough linen of her dress, the black hair falling on either side of her face that seemed sharper without makeup. And the black eyes that watched him, totally unafraid.

She turned away as he moved towards her. She bent over the old-fashioned stone sink and turned the tap on. Drops of water glistened on her hair, made dark patches on her sleeves. Then she reached out to the curtained alcove and found the towel that was there on a hook. It was as if there'd always been just such an alcove in her life, as though she were rooted in the bare white kitchen, Greek, some dark black olive trunk. Suddenly he realised it was a mistake, bringing her to the room.

'I want you to tell me everything,' he said, starting badly and knowing it. 'Everything.'

She turned away again. Again unafraid. She saw the camping-gas stove and brought it out. She brought out a metal Greek coffee pot. Slowly she made coffee and poured it into a tiny cup. Then she found a glass, filled it with water, and took both cup and glass over to the table. She sat down.

Martin stood over her, grabbed her hair. 'I'm going to

find out in the end. You know that, don't you?' He raised his right hand.

But she stared up at him, knowing he wouldn't hit her.

And she was right.

But suddenly he swung his hand down, hitting the cup and the glass. He smacked them against the wall. They smashed. A dark star-shaped stain dripped down on the white.

And there was a flicker on her face. It wasn't fear, just something she was trying to put back into place, in that dark Greek side of her.

And he didn't see what it meant at first.

Until for some reason he thought back to that English school earlier in the day, in Harokopou.

'No . . . No . . . *No.*'

The Charleston on that tiny stage. The tawdry costumes the girls had worn, the ribbons of paper unwinding down their legs. And the strangeness of the dance that was lost somewhere midway between Greece and Europe.

And for some reason too he thought farther back. To Lela, that evening he'd spent with her in the Lykavettos restaurant. The time when she'd been so shocked by Mavromatis, by his girls, by press-stud fasteners . . . That Greek side of her again. Sunlight, a body instinct as against the mechanical, he remembered thinking then . . . A purita . . .

He moved away and leaned against the stone sink, watching her. He walked to the other side of the room, back to a chair, and all the time he watched her.

Then a chill came over him as he knew what he was going to have to do.

He took her by the wrist. He got Halkis' keys from his pocket, and led her through the locked door.

She was surprised by the stifling, all-pervasive air of leather. By the shelf after shelf of books, the rows of bottles, and the pills. He stood there, letting her take it all in, then he led her on to the second room.

Shock began to show on her face at the shape of it, the

shiny hollow pyramid that was set on its side. And the black leather horn, the flower set into its apex . . . Shock which grew stronger as he pushed her ahead of him through the horn, the flower.

Inside they waded waist-deep through the shiny, squashy floor. He showed her the catacombs, the tunnels, the devices. And he shut his mind to those, made himself see only a group of young girls dancing in paper Charleston costumes. It was as far as he would allow his mind to reach into what he was doing.

She was white as he led her back to the first room. He sat her on one of the massive leather chairs. He arranged a table lamp so that it shone onto her lap, and then brought a pile of books from the shelf.

She hissed in her breath at the first photograph, seeing at once that it referred back to that inner room. But she looked down at it, didn't turn away.

The least line of resistance. She could look at photographs. Photographs weren't going to harm her . . . Except that they went on and on and on.

The books were thin, photos bound between covers. There were maybe two-hundred of them in the first shelf alone. It took them nearly an hour-and-a-half to empty it. And then both she and he looked round. And counted . . . There were twenty-three other shelves.

Slowly he stood her up. She was worried at first, until she saw he was leading her back through the locked door to the other apartment, the small whitewashed kitchen.

'Make coffee,' he said.

'What?' It was the first word she'd spoken.

'Make coffee.'

She hesitated, then turned away to the curtained alcove. She made a second cup of coffee and took it, together with a glass of water, over to the table.

As she sat down, he smacked both coffee and water against the wall. Two black stars ran down the whitewash. He took her back again through the locked door.

On and on and on. The locked room alternating with the kitchen . . . And she was slower now, taking more than one-and-a-half hours, nearer two, to empty a shelf of books. She kept looking away from the photographs, and he kept shouting at her, forcing her to look back. She was slower too as she made the cups of coffee he told her to make, her hands trembling . . . waiting, waiting for him to smash the cup yet again.

Instinct told him he was right. Instinct fastened onto her look of sudden relief when he'd smashed the last cup that Halkis possessed. And instinct too made him go out to the market below the apartment and buy a box of fifty cups, a small sack of coffee.

Her face then.

. . . On and on . . . The wall of the kitchen was covered with black stars now. In the leather room, six of the shelves were empty. Twelve hours had gone by his watch. He was taking Benzedrine that he'd found in a drawer, to keep himself awake. And he was shouting at her to keep her awake, shouting often, close to her ear.

And the photographs, the white bodies, the black devices, the awful, awful sameness of them . . . The photographs were beginning to have their effect. Because she began to ward them off. In a low strange voice she began to talk:

'There was our room,' she said, 'the room where Ekaterina, Lakis, and I slept. There was my father's room, and then the courtyard.'

'Yes?'

'It was . . . it was old and crumbling, the courtyard, like the rest of the house. Sometimes it seemed that the only difference between it and the hillside beyond was that its stones had been whitewashed . . . My . . . my father was poor, you see. He only worked three days a week. And his work . . .'

'Yes?'

'. . . His work was to make pastry, the thin sort of pastry they used in the village, *Zacharoplasteion*. He made it on a small machine up at the top of the house. It had a round metal tray, this machine, that used to spin round like a wheel on its side. The tray was sticky with olive oil, and my father used to pour the pastry mixture onto it, and spin it so that it spread very thin, like paper. There was always the smell of paraffin about the machine because of the burners that were underneath it. Pressure burners they were. He pumped up something that looked like a fire extinguisher. Only it wasn't like that, all red and shiny. It was old, an old rusty colour.'

'Yes?'

'One day I remember I was playing in the courtyard,' she said. 'My father was working up in the top room, and there was this explosion. Flames and smoke came out of the window. My father ran out onto the balcony. He swung himself over the edge and he dropped, quite a long way, to the ground. Then he stood and caught the two boys who'd been up there working with him. Caught them. He broke his ankle doing it . . . And then I saw his face. He was looking up at the smoke, the flames, his machine on fire. And he . . . he climbed back up there, hand over hand to the balcony, back into the flames.'

'Yes?'

'There's nothing much to report,' she said. 'He turned off the paraffin tap. He saved the machine and the house. He was burned. But later his hair grew again, and the scars, well, they gathered themselves together . . . But it was when the scars still showed, those first few months. When you looked at him it was as if you were looking through to the rock of a man.'

And instinct, blind instinct, told Martin what to say then:

'Green,' he said. 'The thing that most people say when they come to our house at home is how green it is. Green and, I don't know, peaceful. There are these tall beech trees, you see, on one side of the garden. And at certain times of the year . . . Yes, in May, I remember May most of all, the twelfth, my small daughter's birthday. I remember there were these other girls there too. They were all out on the lawn, wearing their first long dresses, needing space around them suddenly. And my wife was inside the house, playing Haydn and Mozart on the piano for the games they were having. I remember the piano stopping. I remember going in and finding my wife crying, out of happiness. And I remember looking out at those beech trees, the first young leaves, the soft glow of them, and I was filled with this ... this green joy.'

Lela sat quite still, her mouth open, as though she'd been slapped. And it was then, for the first time, that he knew he could win.

Instinct took him on. Instinct made him go over the children's party again, in more detail, describing the party dresses, the girls' names, the games they'd played. He told of the dew coming with the evening, the small footprints on the lawn, the sound of the piano from the shadowy house, the mist rising. , , ,

... And this, this against the terrible photographs he was showing Lela. It was as much as he could manage ... And as much as she could manage too. He knew in a strange way it was affecting her, prising apart the grip she had on her mind. But he knew too that there had to be more.

And instinct came to his rescue again ... The devices in the photographs, the size of them, the unreality of the craftsmanship, the money, that had gone into their making ... Instinct made him enter Lela's madness for a moment and connect the devices with what he was saying.

Because he was talking about the end of the birthday party, about the cars arriving to pick the children up ... And now something caused him to make the cars larger and richer than they had been, make them estate cars, Volvos and Peugeots. And larger, he suddenly realised, because of what they carried ...

Devices ... New gleaming bicycles and tricycles, golf trolleys and supermarket trolleys piled with food. Skate-

97

boards and outboard motors, dinghy paddles, picnic cold-stores, and portable TVs . . .

Instinct took him even farther. It made him fill his house, and the houses of his neighbours at home, with every device he'd ever heard or read of . . . Took him farther still, to the lunatic glitter of Western Europe, the insanity of ease, of over-sufficiency . . . The humidifiers that prevented furniture cracking in over-heated rooms. The high-speed ovens that thawed freezer food in seconds. The factory machines that washed and pounded newly-manufactured jeans until they looked old . . . The tinned dogfood that was flavoured with rabbit . . .

And now, as the cold hard devices continued in the photographs, as the discarded books piled up, and the rubble of broken cups piled up in the kitchen, he knew the connection was made. He talked on and on, repeating himself over and over again . . . And it became a nightmare. The leather room. The bare white kitchen. The fear, hate, and anguish, on Lela's face . . . But all he allowed himself to think about was that he would win.

In the end it wasn't a photograph that broke her.

It was a different book, one he imagined Halkis kept for students he picked up, or sailors perhaps from the Seventh Fleet . . . A tourist book, in English, about Athens.

And it was when he was reading about the Parthenon. Παρθενών. The temple of virgins.

. . . And how in recent years the temple itself had had to be cordoned off. Because its marble floor had been worn away by the feet of tourists.

Tears suddenly ran down Lela's face.

'All right,' she said. 'All right.'

18

He took her back into the kitchen. He placed a chair so that its back was turned to the litter of broken cups and coffee stains. He sat her down, washed her face and hands with cold water, and stroked her hair. He stayed for some time like that, holding her close.

Finally she stopped crying.

'Start at the beginning,' he said. 'Take your time.'

She nodded, moistening her lips.

'It was over six months ago,' she said, 'when I was told I would be needed. It was my English, you see. I'd passed a lot of exams. I passed the Cambridge Higher when I was nineteen.'

'Yes.'

'I was told I'd have to take offices in the centre of Athens. I was told I'd have a lot of memorising to do. Three different files, one on each of three different Englishmen.'

'What?' he asked. 'What?'

'It's quite simple,' she said. 'They wanted an Englishman. One who was an expert shot, and who at the same time was out of work.'

Simple. Quite simple. Put like that, he began to understand.

'The research had all been done before,' she went on. 'And there were a million and a half unemployed in England at that time. It wasn't difficult to find three Englishmen who'd shot at Bisley, won competitions there . . . Unemployed, you understand. Men who'd jump at the chance of a job in Athens if it was presented in the right way.'

'But three? Three men?' Martin asked. 'Why was I the one who was chosen?'

'Your file,' she said. And her voice became flat and mechanical as if quoting from the data she'd memorised. 'It was considered that the pattern of your life-style was uneven. That you worked casually, from one job to the next. Then there was your marriage. That was considered unstable too. There were periods of weeks when your wife left you. It was considered that that would be to our advantage. It was thought that if your present relationship with your wife could be disturbed, if a certain type of man could be introduced to your wife, and she could be persuaded to leave you for another period of . . .'

He reached across suddenly and put his hand over her mouth.

That wasn't simple. Not simple at all.

But gently she broke free. Her eyes were perhaps kinder now as she went on. 'There was another reason, too,' she said. 'Your work, in the Film Industry.'

'What d'you mean?'

'A study was made of the Film Industry,' she said. 'And it was considered that it would be easier to arrange a phoney job around you than around the other two Englishmen. It was found that in films, 80% of scripts written never reached the stage of pre-production. It was found that 60% of scripts in pre-production never reached the first day of shooting. And of those that finished shooting, 50% never achieved a circuit release . . . It was considered that everyone in the Film Industry, from producer down to clapper boy, lived on dreams. Give them a month's salary, a script, and an American voice on the other end of the telephone, and they would believe.'

And Martin nodded. That was true, certainly true. 'All right, I can see that. I can see you taking the offices in Athens. See the fake secretaries in the other rooms, the fake phone calls, the company car . . . But the scripts, thirteen of them, how did you manage those?'

'They were hack scripts, written by a hack writer and never produced,' she said. 'They were bought by a School of Film Technique in London and used on its Television Course.'

'And the Crossplots? The Schedules? They came from the same place?'

'Yes.'

'But,' he frowned, 'those articles in *Variety* about Jake Mallows? And the one in the other magazine too about Dan Leater, Dan.'

'We had pages printed up, and inserted them into real issues.' She shrugged. 'It wasn't really too difficult, when you come to think about it. The most difficult part was all the technical jargon I had to learn. But it was only to hold your interest for a day and a half at the most. And even then we knew you'd be thinking of your wife most of the time.'

'Yes,' Martin said. 'Yes.' And it took him a while to get back to his train of thought. 'But the offices? I mean, the Production Offices? A Film Company? What about the other people in the building? What did they think?'

'To them we were the Fassoulakis Company who made toys,' she said. 'You may remember, our name wasn't up on the door.'

And he did remember.

It was up there, but Mr Elegesis had it taken down. He wanted it done over in gold. Gold, of course.

'The dream, the Film Industry dream,' she said. 'You wanted to believe, and you believed.'

He nodded slowly. The rest of his questions, he knew, were superfluous, but he asked them all the same:

'And the offices, they're empty now, I suppose?'

'Yes. Everything burned or destroyed.'

'And the villa?'

'What?'

'The villa you took me out to. Mavromatis' villa.'

'Well, it wasn't going to be his, was it? There wasn't going to be any way of tracing it back to him.'

101

'No,' he said tiredly, 'I suppose not.'

'I don't know, Mavromatis, he's got friends, high-up, well-connected friends,' she said. 'Probably it belonged to one of them . . . But you're going to find it's been empty all this while, aren't you? Nobody's been there?'

He was silent. Suddenly he had the feeling he was going down a long tunnel, dark, without the faintest glimmer of light at the end.

'Names,' he said then. 'I want names.'

'What names?'

'For God's sake, there was an assassination.' His voice hardened. 'Somebody looked through the sight. Somebody pulled the trigger.'

'*Him?*' She was genuinely shocked. 'You're never going to find him.'

'Why?'

'Don't you understand? Nobody knows him, nobody sees him. He comes into the country and goes out again.'

'Out?'

'Well, he's gone, of course. I don't know how, but gone.'

And he nodded, thinking it was probably true. 'All right,' he said. 'Let's get on to someone you do know. Like Elegesis.'

'I never met him.'

'What?'

'I always contacted him by phone. I rang an exchange. They gave me the number, always a different number.'

'What d'you mean? An exchange?'

'Just a house. A house with a phone.'

'And that'll be empty too now?'

'Of course.'

He hesitated. 'Who *do* you know?' he asked then.

'Just the two girls, the two girls in the office. And the chauffeur.'

'Who are they?'

'I don't know. I only met them a couple of times.'

'And now they've gone underground?'

'Yes.'

'All right, what about Mavromatis?'

'I only met him a couple of times too.'

'But why? I mean, why was he there? In case you got into trouble with me?'

'Yes. He can talk money, any kind of money, and make it sound real.'

'And he's gone underground too?'

'No. I don't think so.'

'What?'

'I don't think he has to.'

'What d'you mean?'

'To know about Mavromatis,' she said, 'you've got to know how he makes his money.'

'You mean, he's rich?'

She nodded. 'I told you, he's got high-up friends, Cabinet Ministers, people like that. And they're going to say what he wants them to say. That he's been with them on his yacht, for example, cruising off the Italian Coast . . . Because it has been cruising there. That sort of thing's in the papers.'

'Yacht? Italian Coast?' He was savage suddenly. 'All right, who else is there? You must know someone else.'

She shook her head.

'Come on,' he grabbed her shoulder, 'you've told me about four people, just four . . .'

'You don't *understand*,' she repeated, her voice high, cracking. 'The way it works, the way it always works, is that everybody knows four people, no more . . . And me, I'm just a girl who sits in an office and talks English. I just don't know any more. You can ask me all night, but I don't.'

And he saw from her face it was true.

But what he didn't see, not at first, was her hand snatching inside his windbreaker.

The razor.

She used it on herself, her wrist.

The blunt blade didn't reach her vein. It made no more than an angry red line, and she stared at it in disbelief.

19

His hands were gentle on her now. He took her into the bedroom and laid her face down on the bed. The light was grey through the window as he stroked her arms, her shoulders, and the dampness that was under her hair. Stroked her on and on, always upwards towards that pulse at the back of her neck. And as he stroked her she shook, a deep uncontrollable shaking that came with every breath.

'In the end . . . the end the police will find you,' she said. 'They'll find out what you know, and I'll be killed.'

'*You?*'

'Yes.'

'No,' he said. 'No.'

She shook harder. 'You've got to think . . . in a bigger way . . . beyond the way you'd normally think . . . anyone would.'

He didn't understand. His mind wouldn't move, only his hands as he loosened her dress and stroked the curve of her back, the points of her spine. He stroked the hollows of her, the soft dark hairs under her arms, the smooth buttresses at the side of her neck. Then he stroked her feet, gently, the hardness of her soles, the flat hard muscles of her flanks.

Gradually they softened. Gradually her shaking slowed, became irregular, stopped. And she slept.

But still he stroked her, unable to sleep himself because of the Benzedrine he'd taken earlier. Stroked the smooth skin that now seemed surprisingly white under her dress, the darkness now lying under the surface . . . And that other darkness, the one that still shook her with fits of trembling even while she slept. The more he stroked her, the more she seemed separate from him, apart.

Until suddenly he realised something as he looked down at

her. That now she needed him as much as he needed her. It was there in front of him. That scar, the angry red line on her wrist. And the shock, the disbelief on her face when she'd been unable to kill herself.

Tiredness at last came to him as dawn light shaped out the window. He took a rug from the bed, lay down on the floor, and slept.

When he awoke, it was late morning, sunlight was streaming around him. And Lela was lying exactly as she'd been last night. Except that her eyes were watching him, moving every time he moved.

They began to make him nervous. The sunlight began to fall back as he looked at her pale frightened face. Until it was again last night, they both seemed to be trapped in the small cell-like room. And the memory of that tunnel came back, the dark tunnel without a chink of light.

He went away to the window. He saw how the sun was almost overhead. He heard the sounds from the market below, the Vespa trucks, the stutter of mopeds.

And then suddenly there was a chink . . . The same light, the same sounds yesterday. At almost exactly this time, midday, when he'd first seen her.

Lela, her back to him, walking away to Kristakis' café.

The café. She'd never reached it. Never picked up the message she was there to collect.

Message . . . He stared at her for a long time, at the red scar on her wrist. He wondered how far it went, how far she'd come over to his side. If she had.

20

But he thought he could trust her.

Half an hour later when he went out with her into the midday rush-hour, she steered him away from the Metro station he'd used yesterday. She told him they should take a trolleybus down towards Kallithea, because the police weren't searching local buses.

And more than that, she told him how to stand like a Greek, how to turn to her and say, '*tee thaylee aftos?*' if anyone spoke to him.

The crossroads at Harokopou was again a howl of cars going between Athens and Piraeus. The café again had its yellow awning lowered, with the chairs and orange-cooler in its shade. And once again Martin stood hidden by the low trees of the ornamental garden, as he watched Lela go into the café, then come out again.

And she had two letters. Two.

They brought them back to the white kitchen with the coffee stains and litter of broken crockery. Lela sat at the table and opened the letters. They were both typewritten, in Greek and, as far as Martin could see, identical.

'What do they say?' he asked.

But she ignored the texts. Instead she looked at the typed references at the top of the sheets. In each case they were the same, *EΔK/852/777/20/30*.

She opened her handbag and got out a street-map of Athens. Then, reaching farther into the bag, she drew out a clear plastic sheet that was fitted inside it, the window in fact of a small ticket compartment.

He saw there were marks along the edge of the plastic sheet. Marks that weren't regular, that had nothing about them that showed they could be used.

Until Lela checked the first three letters of the reference, *EΔK*. Then carefully she laid the plastic sheet on the map, on one particular square of its grid, the E square. And working from the marks that subdivided the plastic, she drew a line.

And another line later, using the second part of the reference, the figures 852, on the numbered side of the grid.

The two lines crossed on the right-hand side of the map. An insert showing Piraeus.

'What's that?' Martin bent close over the exact spot. 'It looks like a harbour.'

'The Zea Marina.' She nodded. 'It's opposite the yacht club.

'Yacht club?' He looked at her. 'So Mavromatis' yacht could be back?'

She didn't answer.

'All right, what's the next part mean?' He pointed to the reference. 'The figures 777?'

'777 means nothing. It's just a filler,' she said. 'Which means in this case there's no street number, no address.'

'Mavromatis' yacht *is* back,' Martin said.

Slowly she nodded.

'And those last two references? 20/30?'

'20.30 hours,' she said. 'Half-past eight this evening.'

'Right opposite the yacht club.' He looked at the map again. 'And Mavromatis is a rich man. Is it a big yacht? Ocean-going?'

'Big. Yes.'

'So they could be going to take you off, out of the country?'

She didn't answer.

He turned back to her, saw the fear that was on her face again, her mouth opening. 'Look, two letters,' she said. 'Two. One yesterday, one today. A repeat . . . And that never happens, a repeat.'

'What d'you mean?'

'There could be trouble,' she said.

21

And there was going to be trouble.

The lights of the yacht club were a little way round the harbour. Nearer, tall masts were swaying under the stars. There were Porsches, Ferraris, parked along the quayside. And a tangle of water-hoses leading away to shifting gang-planks.

Nearer still a huge white stern rose up into the darkness. The *Arkadia*, Mavromatis' yacht. It was big, as Lela had said, the size of a small freighter. Soft needlepoint lights ran the length of it, the gleam of varnish, and dark tinted glass which enclosed the entire lower deck.

And on the upper deck, a tall man in a tartan jacket, looking down at the quay.

Lela, whose fear had grown throughout the day, stared up at him. 'Look at his jacket,' she said.

'Jacket? It's only one of those lumberjack things. What's wrong with that?'

'It's July,' she said, 'the hottest month of the year. How many men d'you see not wearing lightweight suits?'

'What d'you mean?'

'How d'you hide a gun in a lightweight suit?'

And he agreed with her. The man didn't fit into a millionaire's cruising party. Nor was he a seaman. He didn't move like a seaman. And when he lit a cigarette, it wasn't with a seaman's cupped hands.

Martin looked on, past the massive white superstructure to a high foredeck. There were lights up there, bright lights streaming from beneath canvas awnings. And, Martin told himself, it was the place where an owner would sit, for'ard of the smoke from the long squat funnel. But the problem was, he couldn't see.

He drew Lela farther back into the shadows. 'I have to know if Mavromatis is there,' he said. 'Will you do something for me?'

'What?'

'Walk down the quay, past the gangplank, and go on. You'll be able to see then, up to that deck where the bright lights are. You can go on a little way and then come back.'

Her fear grew worse. For a moment he thought her shaking would start again. But then she nodded. She went away.

As she drew level with the *Arkadia*, a cigarette fell through the darkness and hissed in the water. The tall man in the tartan jacket turned, whistled softly.

Another man appeared, a shorter man in a white steward's uniform. They watched Lela and whispered together.

Lela went on, past the sports cars and the tangle of hoses. She came to a light on the quayside, where a group of seamen were talking and smoking. One of them called out to her, but she turned quickly and came back.

As she re-passed the *Arkadia*, Martin suddenly realised the two men on the upper deck were gone. Then he saw a tartan jacket moving quickly down the gangway, saw the tall man stop Lela, talk to her.

But what he didn't see, as they both turned away, was whether Lela was hauled up the gangway, or whether she went willingly.

All he could do was close his eyes and concentrate on that red line, that scar on her wrist.

When he opened them again, he saw the two of them starting along the length of the huge ship. Going, he imagined, up to that brightly lit foredeck, which he couldn't see. He had to get closer.

He looked round. On this side of the *Arkadia* was a box-like motor cruiser. And nearer still, the high curving counter of an old steam yacht. It was a tall thin ship, graceful, its funnel higher than *Arkadia*'s. And it was dark, its decks shrouded in canvas.

He went up the gangway. At its top he seemed to be standing in a long ghostly corridor. There were the canvas covers lashed overhead, the deck sloping down from the high stern to the waist of the ship, and to his right a long row of doors. They were old, beautifully inlaid, Edwardian. At their far end he could see the tiny blue glow from a television set, but no other light.

He went forward. He reached a wide varnished companionway and climbed it. And the deck above, he found, was shrouded in canvas too. But there was a window halfway down it, a square of clear polythene that fastened with studs. He opened it and looked out over the motor cruiser to the *Arkadia.*

He was level with its superstructure now. There was a side-deck and a door open onto a galley. A man was in there, a small man, the steward Martin had seen before. He was bending over his right hand, taping it up with what seemed like a roll of surgical tape.

Then a second man appeared in the galley, a chef, red-faced and angry. *'Où est le tir-bouchon?'* he demanded. *'Le tir-bouchon?'*

Tir-bouchon, Martin knew, was the French for corkscrew. But perhaps the steward didn't understand, or perhaps he didn't care. Anyway he gave no answer. He slid his right hand under his coat and left the galley. He walked forward along the side-deck towards brighter light. The foredeck. Martin still couldn't see what was happening up there. He still couldn't see any sign of Lela or the tall man in the tartan jacket. And he hurried along the length of the dark steam yacht.

He came to another window, one that was level now with the forepart of *Arkadia,* that brightly-lit deck.

It was wide and white. In its centre, a basket chair hung by a chain. And Mavromatis was in it, the huge mass of him plumped onto the cushions, one foot trailing down. The white woman, the one who'd been at the villa that day, was there too, frail and ghostly in a long towelling robe.

111

There were glass tables, and behind them in a wide sweep that covered the entire curving end of the deck, a white fur settee.

Footsteps approached. Far away at the other end of the deck was a chocked speedboat. And by it Lela appeared. The tall man in the tartan coat was gripping her arm, and the steward was close behind.

Mavromatis looked up. His face didn't change, he just asked Lela a string of quiet questions, in Greek. But then he turned his basket chair away, delicately, using just the point of one toe.

And it was that moment, before the other two men closed in on Lela, before she even screamed, that made Martin sure of her, and frightened for her, at the same time.

But frightened as he was, perhaps as frightened as she was, he hauled himself out through the plastic window. Then crossed the flat top of the cruiser towards *Arkadia*'s rail.

He was hidden at first, below that long curving settee. But then, as he climbed the rail, the tall man and the steward spun round. Mavromatis' chair spun too. He slid out of it onto the deck. But by that time Martin had grabbed him, held him in front of him like a shield.

He didn't see the tall man's hand go into his tartan coat. But suddenly there was a pistol, and the long fat pipe of a silencer.

Nobody moved. There was just the basket chair, swinging. Its black shadow swinging on the white deck below. And Mavromatis huge, scented, in Martin's hands.

Then the tall man turned. He said something to the steward.

And Mavromatis was suddenly taut. A strange sound was coming from his throat. Fear.

Of the tall man.

At first Martin's mind couldn't make that leap.

You have to think . . . in a bigger way. He remembered Lela saying.

112

Bigger than a vast white deck, a yacht the size of a freighter, millionaire's quay.

The steward moved towards Mavromatis. And suddenly too many things came together.

The corkscrew.

It was there, long, ornate, taped into the man's right hand. He grunted twice, swung it forward twice, deep. The second time, as if in a dream that became a fragment of itself, Martin saw only the dark blood winding out around the spiral and dropping onto the white deck.

Mavromatis slumped, fell.

The steward scrambled back, out of the line of fire.

And Martin, running, trying to keep with him, knew what it was to die.

The small dark eye of a gun.

He reached the speedboat, its shiny hull suddenly tearing apart into splinters as the gun fired. Warmth, blood on the side of his neck. He threw himself down.

The tall man held the gun out steadily. He moved round steadily to get a second shot, his foot confident as it slid to the side.

But not . . . not a seaman.

His heel caught against an angled support of a davit. He tipped. The gun tipped. His free hand went out, gripped the davit. And it swung, he swinging with it, his body canted half over the rail.

Shock sang through Martin. Shock pushed him on. He reached the tall man. Swung him over.

There was a crunch. A bag of shot falling. The man broke his back on the rail of the deck below. And then fell crookedly on the deck, the pistol skeetering away.

Martin wheeled round.

The steward, corkscrew still taped to his hand, blood on the tape, stood quite still. Then he turned. White-uniformed figures were approaching, crewmen, fit muscled men. They stopped in alarm.

They were between the steward and the quay. He tore

the corkscrew from his hand, dropped it on the deck, and ran, the other way. He climbed the rail, hung by his hands a moment before he dropped. Then the sound of his footsteps went away.

The corkscrew lay there on the white deck.

Mavromatis stared at it. He was half-sitting, one leg under the other, and the front of his shirt was dark and wet. Then the crewmen came over. Two of them picked him up gently, two of them came on to Martin. But then Mavromatis said something, and they left Martin alone.

The crewmen had moved back again. They were standing in a small group by the speedboat. Martin stood by the basket chair, close to Lela. And Mavromatis . . . Mavromatis sat in the centre of the huge white settee. He had a blanket wrapped tightly around him, white too. Except for the black circular stain, which was spreading.

Suddenly . . . Suddenly he laughed.

'Well, Mr Raikes, you've done very well, haven't you? Here you are, still alive, still full of that tiresome Dunkirk spirit. While I . . .' He nodded back along the lit deck towards the quay. 'The final harbour, as those overfed priests keep saying. There's a certain humour to it, you must admit.'

Again he laughed, a tiny echo of that rich brown laugh from before. Martin stood there, appalled. 'But, why?' he asked. 'I don't understand.'

'Ah, yes. All this, the great white yacht.' Mavromatis pointed. 'Here, in my country I am big, it's easy to see that. But . . .' Slowly he nodded the other way, towards the sea. '. . . Out there there's a darkness that stretches a long way. There are people in that darkness, Mr Raikes, people who seldom emerge into the light. And from time to time perhaps they need people like me, for what I know and who I know. But only for a short while. And when they have finished with me, when they decide I am in their way . . .' His hand

114

hovered over the spreading stain on his stomach. '. . . Perhaps standing no more than a metre from where I should be, but still in their way . . . *Tak* . . . They think very simply. A quality I've never admired.'

The white woman stood by his side. She was trembling.

'The darkness out there,' Mavromatis said again. 'Don't fight it, Mr Raikes. You can't anyway. You must keep just within the edge of the light . . . I'm talking about your travelling some way away, you understand, to South America perhaps, the forgotten sunlight there . . . So how much d'you want? Fifty thousand pounds? A hundred thousand? It's no use to me any more . . . Nor my plane. I can get you across the world. I guarantee that.'

Martin shook his head. 'I'll stay here,' he said. 'I have to stay here . . . Proof, cold hard proof. There's been none of that so far.'

'Another simple thinker.' Mavromatis turned to the white woman. 'Isn't it depressing?' He coughed, very slightly. 'All right, proof you shall have. All the proof there . . .' He coughed again. Or rather started the cough. Sweat, fear broke out on his face as he tried to hold back. It was some time before his voice came again:

'But, first things first, if you'll forgive me,' he said. 'A suitable place to die. Wasn't it Oscar Wilde who said that? The right trappings, the right *ambiance*.'

He touched the white woman's sleeve. 'Have you got your book with you?'

'Yes.' She took what seemed to be a fat address book from her pocket.

'So,' Mavromatis said. 'Find the numbers for the following . . . Beethoven, string quartet in B flat major, the *Cavatina* . . . Schubert string quintet in C major, the *Adagio* . . . Then, something more simple. Joseph Haydn, a piano sonata, say, one of the middle Hoboken numbers . . . And then,' he looked up, 'from Fauré's Requiem, the final movement, *In Paradisum* . . . Just for laughs.'

'What about Greek music?' she asked.

'Fuck the Greeks.' They were the only sharp words he said. Then immediately he recovered and turned to Martin. 'And in honour of Mr Raikes here, let's have a snatch of Elgar's First Symphony, the final *coda*. Dear Edward's magnificent motto theme being battered by the stormy brass.' He paused.

'Is that all?'

'I'll see how far I get,' Mavromatis said.

The woman flipped through the book and found the numbers. She was crying.

'Now, wine,' Mavromatis said. 'A bottle of Grands Echézeaux 61, a bottle of Musigny Les Amoureuses 64. And then a newer wine. Clos du Roi, the Beaune Clos du Roi 71. Isn't that the one they still keep in oak vats? I forget now.'

The white woman wrote in her book.

'Two glasses,' Mavromatis said then. 'One for myself and one for Mr Raikes . . . Oh, and we've got a corkscrew.'

The Beethoven came. It hung ghostly over the white deck. White-uniformed stewards came, in a procession, with bottles, glasses, and two silver spittoons.

Mavromatis pointed to them. 'I'm sorry, Mr Raikes, but in my condition it would do me the greatest possible harm to swallow. And I couldn't bear to see *you* swallow the wine, d'you see that? So I wonder if you'd do me the kindness . . . ?'

Martin nodded.

'We'll start with the youngest first, the Beaune wine. I should add that our cellar here on board is perfectly level. Gyroscopically controlled.'

Martin wondered if he were dreaming. He watched the wine being poured. He watched Mavromatis' face, deathly pale now, the veins massing, as he lowered his huge nose over the glass and inhaled. A moment's light came to his eyes. 'Sometimes I think it's not necessary to drink, just to inhale,' he said. But he took a mouthful, ran it round the flapping folds of his cheeks, then spat.

Martin did the same. 'It's very good,' he said. 'Very, very good.'

'Wait.' Mavromatis pointed to the second bottle.

It was poured. The bouquet sniffed, the wine tasted. The Beethoven came to an end and the Schubert began.

'Wine and song,' Mavromatis said. 'There's something missing.'

The white woman undid her white towelling belt. 'Is there something in particular you'd . . .?'

'*Agapi mou*, the greatest pleasure of my life is that soft smooth skin on the inside of your thighs.'

She took his hand and guided it in through the opening of her robe. Behind her the stewards turned their backs, stood quite still. She stood quite still. There was the whiteness of marble about her. Only the tears moved, down her cheeks. And the Schubert, moving through crystal clear chords.

Mavromatis began to cough again. But again he recovered. 'I know what you're thinking, Mr Raikes. It's time for proof now. The proof you want.'

Martin nodded.

'So you shall have it . . . But first I would say this . . . The man, that man who attacked me, will come back. He will bring more of his kind. It's possible that they are waiting at this moment out on the quay . . . So I have arranged that you will leave in the speedboat. You will be taken round to the main port of Piraeus. The boat travels more quickly than any car.'

'Thank you,' Martin said. 'It's . . .'

'. . . There's not much time.' Mavromatis waved him aside. 'Now, the proof. Where shall I begin?'

'At the assassination,' Martin said. 'The core of the thing.'

'So.' The man thought for a moment. 'You leave Piraeus by road. You go back towards Athens. And halfway between Phaleron and the racetrack you will find a Taverna called the Copacabana . . . Yes, the Copacabana, not very original, I'm afraid . . . It stands on open ground. And behind it, along a track, there's a house. The only house in that area that has telephone wires, so you will find it easily . . . Now in that house lives a man called Yarvis. And he is the only one who has proof, definite proof of the assassin. Because as you will understand, the assassin himself left the country two days ago now. Left the same way he came in, on a charter flight, a tourist.'

He paused, fighting for breath. His face was darker suddenly the veins winning. 'The Echézeaux.' He snapped his fingers.

A steward approached. He poured from the third and last bottle, and handed a glass to Mavromatis. The man took it. 'Yarvis. That's just the beginning,' he said. 'There are many things I can tell you. Many, many things . . .'

Panting, his face strangely hollow, Mavromatis levered his nose over the rim of the glass. He breathed in deeply. Then again. And the Echézeaux was too much for him. Suddenly, greedily, he bit into the purple, tasted, swallowed, swallowed.

It took him five minutes to die, his face hidden in the white woman's robe. And by that time the Fauré was playing, boys' voices singing *In Paradisum*.

22

The speedboat thudded over black water. They rounded a point where houses came right down to the shore, and the street lights were chains between them. Then the wind was stronger, there were rows of ships out at anchor, and to their right the entrance to the commercial port. They came in between cranes that were gaunt and silent against wharf-lights, and landed at the steamer dock.

Martin followed Lela as she ran. There was the huge prow of a liner, the slap-slap of dark waves, cobblestones leading to dock gates. And then a wide road, its signs creaking, its newspapers kicking up in the round bowl of wind that was the waterfront. They stopped. There was a car ahead of them, parked at a bus-stop. An old Buick, dusty and battered.

'Come on.' Lela pointed towards it.

'Why? What is it? A taxi?'

'A kind of taxi,' she said. 'A pirate taxi. They follow the bus route into Athens and pick up people at the stops. And people, that's what we need, people around us.'

And there were people. Martin sat wedged in the corner of the old Buick, surrounded by the smell of bodies and cheap cigarettes. He didn't say anything, he let Lela do the talking, and he stared out of the window.

They moved off. Dark streets took them up and away from the harbour, and then downhill again, passing factory walls, the gleam of railway lines, a station. Then Piraeus was behind them, and the sea swung in, dark and wavetorn to their right. They were driving along a flat foreshore, the beginning of a wide bay, with the lights of Athens and the coast resorts ahead.

Later there were other lights, nearer, coming up fast.

Strings of coloured bulbs, and a sign that said COPA-CABANA. Lela leaned forward and tapped the driver's shoulder.

The wind was there again as they got out, and the pump and hiss of beat music, strange on that wide empty shore. The Copacabana had a long windowed front, with lights inside that were strobing across a dance floor. But from the back it wasn't much, no more than a huddle of shacks.

And the house they came to beyond it, two hundred yards away down a dirt road, wasn't much either. It was a single-storey cement building, with the reinforcing wires still sticking up from its flat roof, uncut. Its walls were unpainted, its shutters banged in the wind, there was a courtyard marked out by old oildrums on one side of it, and a bare breeze-block shed on the other. But the phone wires were there, as Mavromatis had said, coming in over scrubland from the road.

Martin walked right round the building. The front and back doors were both locked. There was a light behind the shutters of a corner room, and the sound of a radio playing. He went back to a window on the seaward side, where the shutters were banging wildly, and managed to undo their clasp.

The window behind was cheap, jerry-built. Its glass panes fitted badly, secured by small panel pins, and they too rattled in the wind. He found a piece of thin metal sheet on the ground, and used it to press some of the pins flat. Then, slowly, he took the pane diagonally out through the gap, opened the window, and Lela and he were inside. They crossed a dark empty room and went down a passage towards the sound of the radio.

Yarvis sat at a table, waiting, he knew they were there. But Yarvis was a small man, frightened. He had a thin bald head, a mouth that worked up and down over dentures, and a hole in his shirt that showed a patch of violet vest. Martin got to him. He pulled his jacket back over his shoulders, pinning his arms. Then he looked round at Lela.

120

She found a length of flex that was attached to a table lamp. She tore it free and handed it to Martin. And for a moment he hesitated. Every B-picture he'd ever worked on came back to him as he positioned Yarvis' arms at the sides of the chair, and tied them. But he managed it, even if he wasn't sure about the knots.

Nor, as he looked round the room, was he sure about other things. The cheap furniture, the fairground ornaments, the walls that were painted in bright ice cream colours, pink and green. And the garish picture on the wall, the cowboy riding off into the sunset.

Proof, Mavromatis had said, the proof of the assassination was here. He began to wonder how far the man's sense of humour stretched.

He pointed to Yarvis. 'Ask him,' he said to Lela. 'Ask him who he works for.'

She did, using a harsh Greek voice he'd never heard before.

And Yarvis might have been small, he might have been frightened. But he didn't say anything.

Lela turned back. He knew the look on her face. He'd seen it once before, in the locked room back in Halkis' apartment. And Martin didn't want to go through that again, anything like that. 'I'll take a look around,' he said.

He went through the five rooms that made up the house. He found keys in a drawer, but little else. Then he went out to the shed.

One of the keys fitted. He got the door open. And the first thing he saw was a bench, with tools, spare parts, and rag-waste, along one wall. And the second thing was a car. But surprisingly a new car, an Audi, that had only ten thousand kilometres on the clock. It was locked, he couldn't find a key anywhere, and he went back to Lela.

'It's a garage out there,' he said. 'And there's a car in it, almost brand new.'

'What sort of car?'

'German. An Audi.'

'German plates?'

'Yes.'

She thought for a moment. 'Then we've got him,' she said.

'Got him?'

'Look at him.' She turned back to Yarvis. 'He's frightened isn't he? We've only got to talk about the police.'

'Why the police?'

'Nearly all the cars in this country are imported, well, aren't they? You must have noticed that,' she said.

'Yes.' He hadn't thought about it before.

'Well, what you probably don't know is that there's a hundred-per-cent import duty on them when they come in . . . So, there are men like Yarvis here who drive in across the Yugloslav border late at night. Only they have two-hundred-and-fifty dollars stuck in their passports. And there are certain Customs Men on the border who forget to use their rubber stamps. It's a well-known run.'

She bent over Yarvis again and talked in that harsh Greek voice. And this time he answered, sweating, licking dry lips.

When he'd finished, Lela translated:

'He brought the car in ten days ago,' she said. 'It was for the usual people, the same people he always works for. But there was one difference. It wasn't just the car he had to bring in. There was an electric polisher on the back seat . . .'

'. . . A what?'

'A polisher, an electric floor polisher, he said. He had to bring that in too.'

Martin stood there for some time, thinking. Then he looked at Lela again. 'Ask him where the car keys are,' he said.

They were hidden behind a tile in the bathroom. Martin took them out to the garage and unlocked the car.

There was nothing on the seats, on the floor, or in the lockers, they had all been swept clean. But when he went round to the back of the car and opened the boot, he found what he was looking for.

There were three separate items. The first was a small duffel-bag that contained a thermos, the remains of a packed meal, and a Michelin Guide to Greece.

The second was a bundle, a pair of overalls wrapped around scuffed black shoes and a Texaco cap. But the overalls were unusual. They had pads, thick pads of foam rubber, sewn into the inside of the elbows. And in the pocket was a left-hand glove that was padded too, on the outside, like a batsman's glove.

And finally, hidden under a rug, the floor polisher. A large one, a commercial machine.

He looked down at it for a moment. Then he looked across to the workbench by the garage wall. He went over and examined the spare parts that were on it. And he found something that didn't belong to a car. It was an electric motor, with a tubular plastic tank fitted above it.

The insides of an electric floor polisher.

He found tools, went back to the car-boot, and started working on the polisher. It came apart in two sections. The lower section where the brushes were, and the longer tubular section above it.

Inside the lower section he found a parcel containing $25,000 in used notes.

And inside the upper section, wrapped in a heavily padded slip-cover, he found a rifle. A Match Rifle, built onto the old P14 pattern. Identical to the one he'd found at Boudapesti 3.

23

He went back into the house.

'What's the matter?' Lela looked up. 'D'you want me to ask him more questions?'

'No,' Martin said. 'I want time. Time to think.'

'So?'

In answer he turned and switched off the light. Then he crossed to the window and drew back the curtains. 'Just keep watching that road,' he said. 'And come for me if you see lights or anyone moving. They're going to work out that Mavromatis talked to us, aren't they? And then they're going to make a list of everyone he knew.'

Once again he went back to the garage. He closed the door and stared down at the car-boot. He knew that everything inside it counted. Everything.

The rifle.

You know about rifles, Halkis had said. *He's not going to be the man of the popular thriller, is he? The man who opens a briefcase and screws together a small gun that looks like a drainpipe.*

And that he wasn't.

A gun that looked like a drainpipe. It was going to be accurate at shorter ranges only. Perhaps two shots in three.

Which gave that particular man two choices. He could miss a third of the time. Or he could retire and write thrillers.

And the reason was simple . . . A hand gripping a bare metal barrel.

Martin thought back to his Bisley days.

The long range rifle. And its characteristic known as 'barrel jump'. This was a series of vibrations which began at the moment the trigger was squeezed and the striker moved forward. A series of vibrations which built up at the explosion, built up even more as the bullet left the barrel, at something approaching 3,000 feet per second. And that bullet had to leave the barrel at an exact and calculated point in its vibrations. Every bullet. An absolute consistency.

Which was why, when you'd finished paying for your Schultz & Larsen barrel, you paid one of the very few gunsmiths who could do the job for you, to 'bed' it into a heavy P14 stock. And this 'bedding' took weeks. It involved, among other things, making bearings out of hornbeam, fitting them into the draws of the rifle and the barrel re-inforce, and then ensuring that the barrel was floating from the re-inforce forwards . . . Floating. Untouched by hand.

Which was why a long range rifle was fully 4 ft 6 inches long. Why it had a barrel 3 ft long, a telescopic sight 2 ft long. Why it weighed over 15 lbs. And why it couldn't be knocked or damaged in any way.

He picked it up, the rifle, and felt the balance of it, smelt the familiar smell of oiled wood. Then he looked down at the padded slip-cover and saw the pocket that was set into the side of it. He opened it and found four chargers of ammunition, Raufoss Match. One of them with empty cases.

He picked them up. The brass was cold under his fingers. He thought about the fingers that had last touched them, slotted them into the breech.

The man.

He'd flown out two days ago, Mavromatis had said, on a charter flight. And come in the same way, probably only three or four days before that. Probably a weekend tourist return flight.

And the rifle? The rifle that was 4 ft 6 inches long, and weighed 15 lbs? How had that come in?

. . . The answer was the Audi, the nearly new German car that had been brought in over the border by a man called Yarvis. A regular run. Probably Yarvis hadn't even known he was bringing in the rifle. No. Definitely he hadn't known. A man who had a house with broken shutters? Windows that were secured only by panel pins? A man who'd shown the hiding-place of the car keys as soon as he'd been asked?

So the gun had been hidden. Where? In the floor polisher? Then why was the polisher mechanism over there on the workbench? Why had it been stripped out *after* it had arrived?

Work it out. The polisher had been intact when Yarvis had brought it in. Therefore it could have been examined by the Customs man on the frontier. Just a favour, Yarvis would have said, a favour for a friend. Perhaps he'd had to pay extra. Perhaps he'd driven on into Greece wondering how he could claim the money back on his expenses.

And the gun hadn't been in the polisher then. It had been hidden in the car. Somewhere deep. A compartment, a padded compartment, perhaps in the sills.

Then why the polisher?

Martin looked at it, lying in the car boot. He looked at the duffel-bag, the overalls, the shoes, the padded left-hand glove, the Texaco cap.

Everything counted.

He saw the man again, flying in on that charter flight, surrounded by tourists with their duty-free bottles and cigarettes. He saw the hotel they all went to, second class, nothing conspicuous.

And then, perhaps on the second or third day, the day that Dr Aloysius Grivela was due to drive through the streets, he saw the man leave that hotel. He saw him come out here. Here, to this garage.

Because someone from the organisation would have made that possible, would have got Yarvis out of the way first. And then the man would have come. He'd have let himself into the garage and locked the door behind him.

The rifle. He'd get it out of its hiding-place. It would be

in its padded slip-cover, but even so he'd examine it, the barrel and sight, for any slight marks. He'd check that the bolt-action was smooth, he'd check the trigger, first and second pressures. Then he'd find tools from the workbench, just as Martin had done, and strip the mechanism from the polisher. He'd fit the rifle and the dollars inside. He'd put on the overalls, the Texaco cap, and the shoes. And finally he'd put the thermos and the packed meal he'd brought with him into the duffel-bag.

And the Michelin? The red Michelin Guide? Everything counted, Martin knew that. But he couldn't see the reason for it at the moment, and he left it go.

He concentrated on the man, driving out of the garage. It would be perhaps 12.15 p.m., about three quarters of an hour before the siesta began. He'd drive back into Athens, towards the sloping streets of the new business section. Towards the avenue and Boudapesti Street.

It would be an area that he knew well, one that he'd visited before, perhaps two or three times, working out angles of fire, ranges, and the direction of the sun. He'd park the Audi now in one of the streets he'd picked out. He'd take the floor polisher out of the car and put it over his shoulder. Then he'd walk to an office building, one that was perhaps next to Boudapesti 3, or one that was farther away. He'd go up to the roof, a low roof, where the angle wouldn't be against him. He'd find a place in the shade, and he'd wait. For one o'clock, when the building below him would be empty.

Then he'd unscrew the polisher. He'd take out the dollars and put them in his pockets. He'd take the rifle out of its slip-cover and go over to the corner of the roof. Then he'd put on the padded left glove, the glove that was going to be resting on the parapet. And he'd find his position.

The overalls. Martin saw the white dust on their thickly-padded elbows, the sweat-marks under their arms. And the scuffed shoes. He saw the man settle himself slowly, taking his time, until his position was natural, his weight evenly spread between both elbows, his cheek just behind his right thumb.

And for a moment Martin had a strange thought. That perhaps this man had once shot next to him at Bisley. Perhaps they'd met. Because there were very few Match Rifle shots in the world. There were very few places where you could learn Match Rifle shooting. But wherever you learned, if you were good, there was only one place you made your way towards.

The Stickledown Range at Bisley. A thousand yards . . . Again Martin picked up the rifle. On his day he'd been able to score 46 out of 50 there. And perhaps this man too. 6 bulls and 4 inners. 6 shots inside a 30 inch circle. At over half a mile.

Not that this man would attempt anything like that range now, from the roof. Perhaps a fifth of it, perhaps 200 yards.

But one thing was certain, he'd need the same degree of accuracy, probably more. The head and shoulders of a man. In a moving car.

Martin winced as he looked through the sight. He didn't want to think of the view through that 12x telescope as those high-velocity rounds went in. Instead he looked above the eyepiece to the adjusting screws, the two small milled knobs.

The range. How had the man measured that?

He lowered the gun and looked away. And again he caught sight of that red book, the Michelin Guide.

Then he remembered. The inserts on almost every page, the large-scale maps of towns.

He opened the Guide at the map of Athens, the page that included the avenue. And then he found them, the pinpricks and tiny pencilled curves made by a draughtman's compass. On the scale below the map that was measured in hundredths of metres. And on the map itself, the avenue.

The pinprick there was a little away from Boudapesti Street, perhaps two buildings away from Boudapesti 3. There were two pencilled curves, one at 200 metres, and one at 250. And the spot where Grivela had died, where his car had been slowing for the crossroads, was at the 250 metre mark. This man was good then. Very, very good.

And Martin saw him again, turning from the Guide to the first of the adjustments on the telescopic sight, the elevation. Then he saw him testing the wind and moving the second adjustment, the wind gauge. He saw him choosing a mark on the avenue below, trying four or five practice shots with an empty rifle. Squeezing the trigger, first pressure, then second, his right hand doing most of the work, his left, helped by the rifle sling, gripping a little less tightly, the cap vizor low over his eyes. And all the while trying to slow down his breathing, the pumping in his head.

And then, not satisfied, but as satisfied as he would ever be, he saw him reach out for the first charger of Raufoss ammunition. He saw him slot the charger into the breechguide and press the rounds home. Five rounds. He saw him push the bolt forward, put the safety catch on.

And finally he'd wait. Not for two o'clock, when Dr Aloysius Grivela's motorcade was due. But for a few minutes before two.

Because then a black Mercedes would draw up at the top of Boudapesti Street. And through his telescopic sights the man would see two figures inside, a chauffeur, and Martin. He'd see Martin get out, walk down towards Boudapesti 3, unlock the door, and go in.

. . . A few minutes before two . . . Two of those minutes, say, would be taken up by Martin finding the lift was out of order and walking up to the third floor. A minute or two more finding out that the office was empty.

And that was enough, Martin suddenly realised. That he should be in an empty building where he had no right to be. A building moreover with one window open. And below that window, a second Match Rifle, placed on a ledge.

But that he should have sat down in that office, wrapped up in thoughts about Dan Leater, not realising the building was empty. That he should still have been there when the shots were fired. More, that he should have leaned out of the window then and shown himself . . . That must have been too much for the man to hope for. He must have crawled back over the roof then, hidden the rifle and the money once again in the polisher. And waited with certainty growing inside him. The certainty of being able to spend a million dollars.

And then that certainty fading. Because Martin hadn't been found. The office buildings hadn't opened again after the siesta. The streets had been cordoned off.

The long night. The sweat on the man's overalls, the stale crusts in the packed food wrappers, the cold coffee in the bottom of the thermos. Martin saw him moving from hiding-place to hiding-place, ventilator shafts, store rooms. Perhaps taking the polisher with him, perhaps leaving it in one place.

And then the light of morning. The same morning that Martin had seen, just two buildings away. The crowds outside in Boudapesti Street, but the police cordons gone. So the man had left, just walked out of the building with the polisher. He'd driven back here to this house, this garage. He'd changed back into his tourist clothes, and gone back to his hotel.

And the next day he'd flown out. Gone.

Martin turned to the parcel then, the $25,000 in used notes.

Kept in case of emergency. And abandoned when the emergency never came.

That man wasn't going to be found.

Martin stood in the garage, thinking. And then he heard it, the sound from the house. But not a footstep, or a car drawing up. The sound of a telephone.

It grew louder as he ran back to the darkened room where Lela waited, tense, by the open window. Then it stopped.

A moment later, it started again.

'Don't answer it,' Martin said. 'Leave it alone.'

130

But then he heard a scuffling, feet banging against furniture . . . Yarvis, he'd broken free.

The phone was snatched up. Yarvis was shouting down it. Martin got to the light-switch, clicked it on, swung round.

But Yarvis was no longer shouting. His face was servile. *'Ton Anglon,'* he said. *'Ton Anglon. Malista.'*

'What's he saying?' Martin asked.

'The Englishman,' Lela said.

'What?' And he stared. Yarvis was holding the phone out now, to him.

He took it.

'Mr Raikes?' A man's voice said. 'Elegesis.'

24

'You found the gun,' Elegesis said. His voice was without accent or inflection. Grey. There were no questions, just statements.

'The gun, yes,' Martin said.

'I see. Well, that can only help us now.'

'Help you?'

'Yes, it's ironical in a way, isn't it? The gun in the hands of the right person.'

Martin stood quite still. He hadn't thought of that.

'We've taken care of everything else,' Elegesis went on. 'We've arranged for Mavromatis' yacht to leave Piraeus and cruise abroad. We've withdrawn all our units from the streets. There's no one left in Athens that you would remember. Or even that the girl would remember. And the girl is dead. Every time you look at her, remember that.'

Martin turned. Lela was close to him, close enough to hear.

'The police have now come in from the streets too,' Elegesis said. 'The streets of Athens, that is. They're following a very strong lead in Saloniki . . . So I'd say the way is clear for you to go to the British Embassy.'

'The Embassy? You mean, you *want* me to go there?'

'Yes. With the gun. We want you to confess to the assassination of Dr Grivela. It's the simplest way now.'

There was a pause.

'You're out of your mind,' Martin said.

'No.'

The word hung there, quiet, confident, in the silence.

'Your house,' Elegesis said then. 'Your house in England among the trees.'

'What?'

'The living room. That rather nice L-shaped room. And the piano by the window where your wife plays Mozart and Haydn sonatas . . . To the right of the piano there's a stripped pine chest, isn't there? With the stereo-unit that you've carpentered so neatly into the top drawer? . . . And underneath the chest, between its flat base and the carpet, there are . . . letters . . . Your wife hides them there. They're letters she's never wanted you to see.'

'What?' Martin said. '*What?*'

'Forget the letters. I'm only trying to tell you that we know about the room, everything about the room,' Elegesis said. 'Let's move on, shall we? Past the pine chest to the bookshelves . . . And the lowest bookshelf, where you keep your boxes of coloured slides.'

A chill ran through Martin.

'You're quite a photographer, aren't you, Mr Raikes? Those *contre-jour* shots of the children? The ones I liked most were of Pru and Simon when they were, what, three and one years old? Simon holding the striped tiger that was his favourite toy then . . . It's not any longer, is it? It's a James Bond car.'

The chill spread. Martin couldn't breathe.

'Your wife and children are back in the house now, I don't know if you've heard,' Elegesis went on. 'And I suppose you could phone them. It would mean exposing yourself here in Athens, of course, but you could still do that . . . But then what? I mean, even if you were believed, if the word of some fanatic political killer were believed, what would happen? It's England, remember. The authorities would place a policeman outside the door, two policemen at the most . . . And you see, we could send a unit, two, three units, just like that.'

Martin was nothing, nothing. Darkness looking out from a dark skull.

'What's the time now? Ten p.m.?' Elegesis asked. 'Let's call it twelve hours, shall we? Ten a.m. tomorrow. By that time you're to walk into the British Embassy, with the gun,

133

and confess to killing Dr Grivela. Otherwise I shall pick up the phone and make certain arrangements . . . Oh, and one more thing. It's only fair that you choose. Which one of your children d'you want killed? Pru or Simon?'

25

The darkness was still there in his head. And now there was a rushing too. He saw the photograph, the coloured photograph Elegesis had talked about. Pru and Simon at home, the striped tiger Simon was holding, the sun coming through the beech leaves, the garden swing.

Then the darkness cleared, the rushing went away. He heard the sound of the wind coming over the flat foreshore, the banging of shutters. He saw the room where he stood, the garish ice-cream colours of the walls, the picture of the cowboy and his horse cut from the magazine, the comic books . . . Yarvis.

He grabbed Yarvis and slammed him heavily down onto a chair.

'What are you going to do?' Lela asked, afraid.

And he didn't know.

'It's no good getting rough with him,' she said. 'He's just a small man. He delivers cars. He . . .'

'Ask him,' he said.

'Ask him what?'

'About the car. How he goes about picking up cars like that. Who he contacts. Who he knows.'

'It won't do any good.'

'Ask him.'

She did so, standing between him and Yarvis, translating the questions and then translating the answers back.

It seemed there was a phone-hall in Athens, a place where working men went to make calls. It seemed there was a man there who put work Yarvis' way. Car delivery jobs, and small sealed packages he delivered to hotel rooms.

'Sealed packages,' Lela turned back to him. 'Small sealed packages. I told you, it isn't any good.'

But he didn't answer. He was thinking about the car in the garage outside, and the rifle in its boot. The most important sealed package of them all.

And then, something that Halkis had said, last night when they'd talked . . . *The man who killed Grivela, how many people d'you think there are like that in the world? He gets paid a million, perhaps millions.*

Millions . . . That man wasn't going to leave anything to chance. Anything to do with the rifle. Somewhere along the line he had to have a contact. Someone in Athens who came out here first to check that the car had arrived intact.

He turned back to Lela and Yarvis. And he led up to it slowly:

'Ask him about the job. Ask him if it was special, if he got paid over the odds.'

The answer was no.

'Ask him how he got paid.'

An envelope in a left-luggage locker.

'And how he handed over the car keys.'

The same way.

'All right. Ask him if anyone contacted him, by phone, say, wanting to know details of the trip from Germany.'

Again the answer was no.

But Yarvis was lying.

Martin didn't let it show that he knew. He went on in exactly the same voice: 'Ask him if anyone came out to check over the car. Here, after he'd brought it to the garage.'

Again, no.

And again Yarvis was lying.

Martin thought for a moment. Then he asked Lela to go out to the car and bring back the gun.

He stood there, waiting, staring at the lurid coloured walls, at the magazine picture facing him, the cowboy, the horse, and the sunset . . .

Suddenly he moved. Suddenly Yarvis' blood was on his

136

knuckles, Yarvis' mouth was split and puffy, and Lela was pulling at him, shouting in his ear.

He walked away to the centre of the room. Gradually his breathing slowed. 'Show him the gun,' he said. 'Tell him what it was used for, and who died. Ask him if he's listened to the radio in the last few days.'

Yarvis was frightened then, really frightened. He sagged in his chair, and words spilled out of him.

Yes, there'd been unusual things, many unusual things, about this job. They'd started when he'd crossed the border from Yugoslavia. A car had crossed behind him, not a police car, and had stayed behind him through the Customs queue, just to make sure.

And, yes, other things. The fact that he'd been told to bring the car here to his house, instead of delivering it as he usually did. Bring it here, and wait. Then a man had phoned. Not the same man as just now, a different man. He'd told Yarvis he was to go away on holiday. He was to take the boat to Poros, one of the islands. A hotel had been booked for him there, and a boat ticket on a certain morning.

But Yarvis hadn't left that morning. He'd waited. Because of the unusual things. Unusual enough to do him some good. He'd decided to stay around and keep his eyes open. There was a way of making money out of things like that, even if it meant a short phone call to the police.

So he'd waited here, in this room by the window. And he'd seen a car. It hadn't come by the coast road, past the taverna, but the other way, the track inland. An expensive car, a BMW, new, but with one wing dented. It had waited out there, waited a long time. No one had got out. Then it had driven away. And half an hour later Yarvis had got another phone call. The same voice . . . Unless he got the hell out to Poros, he was going to find himself cemented into the new yacht marina they were building out at Glyfada . . . He'd gone. Straight away.

137

'And then?'

Nothing else. Nothing.

The man was crouching down on his chair now, his eyes rolling with fear. Martin believed him.

He stood by the window, thinking for some time.

'What do we do now?' Lela asked.

'We go to this phone-hall in Athens and meet his contacts,' Martin said. 'And we spread the news around.'

'News?'

He went over to the Match Rifle. 'About this. It seems to have quite an effect. Well, doesn't it?'

He slid the rifle carefully back into its case. Then he took Yarvis by the arm and led him out to the car. He sat him in the front seat, shut the car door, and started looking round the garage.

Finally he found what he was looking for, what he knew a man like Yarvis would have, a pair of Greek registration plates. He fitted them on to the Audi in place of its original German plates. It wasn't much, but it was the best he could do.

The irony, Elegesis had called it. That he, Martin Raikes, misfit, marksman, and the rest of it, was going to be driving around Athens with a long-range rifle and $25,000 in his car boot.

But there was no time to think of that now.

. . . Pru and Simon, asleep in that house in England among the trees.

It was now half-past ten.

There were eleven-and-a-half hours to go.

26

They were walking under arches, the portico of an old scarred building. There were posters, torn political posters, everywhere on the stonework, the words, OXI, NAI, ZHTΩ, and stern military faces staring down from them. And there were stalls too under the arches, tiny stalls that were no more than lit glass cases set up on trestles. They had coins and secondhand watches laid out in them. Men kept approaching from the shadows and whispering one word. And the word, Lela told him, was gold.

They were walking close together, Martin with his right wrist tied to Yarvis' left with a belt, Lela just a pace ahead. Then at the end of the portico she stopped and pointed. Round the corner was an entrance, a smeared glass door, with a sign above it that said, OTE. They went in, and through a second glass door they saw the phone hall.

It was a long grey-painted room with a bare wooden floor. There was a row of hardboard booths along one side. And on the other a large old-fashioned switchboard where a crowd of men stood, waiting for their numbers to be called. Their voices were low. There was a feeling of the small hours. It was the dimness, the flickering neons. And the grey walls and booths, where every square inch seemed to have been scribbled on.

Lela talked to Yarvis. Then she turned.

'There's the man,' she pointed, 'standing over there behind the big man in the chair.'

Martin saw them both, but it was the sitting man who took his eye. A huge white slab of a man, his head shaved, his mouth dribbling.

'He's a little crazy,' Lela said. 'They let him sit here like

that because he likes the sound of the phone bells. Yarvis'
man looks after him.'

'What's his name? Yarvis' man?'

'Fotcheion. And the crazy one's called Blood Bank.'

'Blood Bank?'

'Yes,' she hesitated, 'Fotcheion rents him out. At the
hospital you can get 1200 *drachs* for 50 ccs of blood.'

Martin stared then, at the man's dead whiteness, his slow,
almost underwater movements. It was a moment before he
could turn back to Lela and think out what they were going
to do.

'Look,' he said, 'you'll have to go over there, close to
this Fotcheion man, close enough to hear what's said. And
before that, you'll have to spell it out to Yarvis, exactly
what it is he's to say.'

She nodded.

'It goes like this . . . The Englishman came to see him,
the Englishman who's been on all the radio bulletins. He
found out about the gun, the assassin's gun, hidden in the
Audi, and now he's going to the authorities. He's going to
tell them about the Audi, how it came into the country,
who drove it in, and who fixed up the job.'

She nodded again.

'All right. Now, if he says that, *just* that and no more,
then you're to give me a nod . . . And Yarvis can go free.
He can leave the building, pass me here in the hallway, and
I won't make a move to stop him. He can disappear.'

It happened, just as Martin had said. The two men talked.
Lela nodded. And then Yarvis left, hurried out into the
night.

And other things happened too. Fotcheion became frightened. He moved round to Blood Bank's side and whispered
urgently into his ear. Then he got him up onto his feet.

Lela came out. She paused only a moment at Martin's
side. 'They're leaving,' she said. 'I'm going to get the car.'

They were there through the car windscreen now, Fotcheion and Blood Bank, almost a block ahead. Blood Bank a huge shambling figure, his hands out, his feet bending strangely as he walked, as though sinking down into the hard pavement like sand. And Fotcheion urging him on, darting around him like a dancing master with a bear.

The streets were narrow and dark, their rooftops jumbled against a glow ahead. Then the glow became brighter, became Akademias Street, according to Lela, near the centre of Athens. It was up there on the other side of a square, with its brightly lit cafés and flower shops. But this side of the square was commerce, grey and peeling. There were quays where buses pulled up, and the cafés were set back into the shadowy entrances of office buildings.

Suddenly Fotcheion and Blood Bank disappeared through a doorway.

Lela put her foot down, drew up by the curb, and leapt out. Martin followed her. They went in through the doorway and found themselves staring at a noticeboard of Company names. They stood there for a moment, and then they heard the sound from above. Blood Bank's slow padding footsteps as he climbed stairs. They followed.

The stairs were stone, with iron banisters. Through them, when they were almost level with the third floor, they saw Fotcheion and Blood Bank go away down a dim passage and stop by a door. They knocked on it. The door opened, and Martin drew back. He could see their two pairs of feet, and a third pair, inside the doorway, wearing carpet slippers. The carpet slippers led the others inside.

They waited. There were raised voices now coming through the door, a voice that Martin took to be Fotcheion's, and another the man in carpet slippers, trying to calm him down. Lela signalled Martin to stay where he was, and she went down the passage towards the door. She stayed there for some time, listening. Then she came back, motioning him to go down the stairs, and out the way they'd come.

They sat across the street, in the hallway of another building. There were café tables there, the smell of carbolic and cheap cigarettes, and the smell of coffee that a young boy brought, swinging it on a metal tray that was like a birdcage.

Lela sipped hers. 'He's a lawyer,' she said. 'Δικηγόρος, it was on the nameplate on his door.'

'Lawyer? You mean, they've gone to him for help? *Those* two?'

'No. From what I heard, he's part of it, part of the car-delivery business. And he was worried, very worried about the gun in the car, though he tried not to show it.'

'So?'

'So he said he was going to phone.'

'Who?'

'I don't know. All he said was he'd phone, and they'd have to wait.'

Wait . . . Martin looked at the dim arcade around him. At the men with frayed cuffs sitting at damp metal tables. At the doorways with their jumbles of signs, First Floor, Second Floor, small arrows pointing to small deals. . . . A lawyer in carpet slippers. A man called Fotcheion who rented out a man called Blood Bank. He was wasting his time. There wasn't going to be anything for him here.

And it was eleven-fifteen now. There were just ten hours and forty-five minutes to go . . . The smell of carbolic came back. The boy who'd brought the coffee was now mopping down the floor. Martin watched the mop-circles spreading away from him, down the arcade.

Then he saw it, drawing up across the street. The car, the BMW with one dented wing.

And he knew he was no longer wasting his time. It was a new expensive car, as Yarvis had said. And the man who got out was expensively dressed, in a dark loose-fitting suit. He was a powerful man, broad-shouldered, but he moved lightly on the balls of his feet. The assassin's contact man.

He went into the building opposite, where the lawyer had his office.

And ten minutes later, he came out again.

27

Martin was running, hard, at full stretch, among the lights and cafés of Akademias Street. Behind him Lela was some way back in the Audi, trapped in a snarling traffic queue. And now, insanely, he was chasing the moving BMW, on foot.

Shop windows flew past him, and tourists' faces, startled as they turned. He cannoned into them, pushed them aside, smashed his way through a line of café chairs. There was this rage inside him now, as if he were trying to burst his way through the city, the shiny walls, the pavements, and the hard night sky.

Ahead, far ahead, came the stab of brake lights, a row of them at a crossing. And among them, he knew, was the BMW. He ran on, forcing his feet harder, faster. Then he saw the car, the metallic blue of it, still far off, two blocks away. But it was winking left, edging left to cross the stream of traffic.

The lights changed at the crossing. There were hoots, a tangle of cars. Martin chanced losing a second, chanced a look round. His side of the road was clear. He ran across, and then suicidally jumped, lurched his way through the sudden storm of brakes and headlights in the far stream. He reached the pavement. The BMW was still at the crossing, winking left. Martin ducked left too, up a dark street.

It was a hundred-and-fifty lung-bursting yards to the next corner. He got there, just in time to see a flash of metallic blue, a block away, going uphill.

There was no more strength in him, but he ran, reached the steep street, shuddering, sawing for breath. He saw the BMW far above him on the hillside, bouncing in a sudden lurch of springs and headlights as it crossed a traverse. And

144

went on, two blocks farther up the hill, before turning right.

He could no longer run, he could hardly walk, and he went slowly up to that high traverse, knowing that when he got there it would be useless . . . And it was. The street was long and empty, apartment blocks gleaming blue under cold blue lamps.

Then the rage came back to him, the rage at this hard city, polished smooth, without a crack . . . And it began to show him things, began to narrow the chances.

The street. It was high up on the steep hillside, there were no streets uphill to the left, but flights of steps. And while to the right there were streets, the rage in Martin, the logic, told him there was no point in driving farther up a hill than was necessary, and then driving back down again.

None of which meant that the man lived in the street. It could be that he'd driven along it to another farther round the hillside . . . But the chances were narrower. Martin decided to look at every car, in this street, and in any other that went on from it at the same level.

He did so, checking first the cars at the curbside, and then the ones he found parked in underground garages. Because each apartment block, he discovered, had its own garage, approached by a curving concrete ramp.

Halfway down the street on the right, he suddenly found what he was looking for. It was a brightly lit garage, white tiled, with blue tiled numbers over the parking bays. And there, among Cadillacs and Mercedes with CD plates, was the BMW.

It was in bay Number 11, there were sixteen bays in all. He went back outside and looked up at the front of the building . . . Eight floors. And, say, two apartments on each floor . . . Which meant apartment Number 11, on the fifth floor.

He returned to the street corner and went back down the hill a little way. His first thought now was to try and find Lela. He knew she would have seen him from behind as he'd run across Akademias Street in the sudden flurry of

145

headlights. He knew she would have seen him take the first of the side streets that led uphill. And he hoped she'd come looking for him.

He waited. The first three cars he saw moving below him he didn't recognise. But the fourth, as it dipped down to cross a traverse and showed its shape behind its lights, he knew was the Audi. He ran down towards it, waving his arms.

Lela picked him up. She drove him back to the corner and slowly along the street where the man's apartment was ... Until Martin grabbed the handbrake. He stopped the car and made her reverse back.

Because suddenly he remembered.

The assassin's contact man. He knew the car, the Audi. He'd come out to check it over at Yarvis' house, before the assassin had arrived.

And something else he remembered too, something Yarvis had said ... The man had waited half an hour, parked out on the dirt track, watching Yarvis' house. Half an hour, and then driven away.

Martin knew now that he was near people who took great care. Workmen's phone-halls, men who sold gold in the shadows were things of the past. The apartment blocks stretched ahead of him, polished and close together, with their ramps, their underground garages, their cars with CD plates ...

He turned to Lela. 'Wait here,' he said. 'I'll do this one on my own.'

He got out and walked down the street.

28

From twenty yards away he saw the closed-circuit camera in the porch, directed down onto the row of apartment bells. He stayed well clear of it, and looked back along the front of the building for another entrance. There was only one, the garage. And once again he walked down the sloping ramp.

He was careful now, making as little noise as possible. He went past the BMW and the row of cars next to it and came to an entrance between two pillars, a lift. But it was locked, with a heavy steel keyhole set into its metal door. He turned. To his right, in the shadow, he saw where the white tiles of the garage ended. There was plain cement there, and a third entrance, a tunnel. It had a sign over it, Θυρωρός. Somewhere Martin had seen that word before, or heard it before, he was almost sure it meant *concierge*. And he followed the sign, down the dark tunnel.

He came out in deep shadow. Apartment blocks, the backs of apartment blocks, towered on every side. The light from their windows made strange patterns on a backlot the size of a tennis court. Just ahead of him he saw the roof of the underground garage. It was a flat square of concrete with ventilators set into it, shiny plastic mushrooms that glowed faintly in the light from below. And beyond was waste ground. Building materials had been dumped there, and cast-out furniture. A cane rocking chair that sat strangely on a heap of white sand.

He turned to his left. Close to the building he'd just come through was a small courtyard. The *concierge*'s courtyard, Martin knew it from the battered trunk outside the door, and the cheap doll lying out on the flagstones. He tried the door. It was locked. The sound of television came from the window next to it. Martin went on past the courtyard to a buttress that stuck out at the far end of the building. There were shadows beyond, and he wondered if he would find another entrance there.

But he didn't. All he found was gleaming metal. Twin rails that rose up on the building, attached to the wall, and some sort of buffer arrangement at their base. He didn't understand what they were, all he knew was that they didn't help. There was nothing for him here, no entrance, and no way round the apartment block. He was in a corner, formed by one smooth wall and the next. He turned, and was about to go back the way he'd come . . . when the first shot came.

It went through his sleeve, taking a chunk out of the concrete wall. And the second whined past his head.

White dust was in his mouth and on his face. And he fell, hands out in front of him, smelling the smell of earth, of concrete as he found the corner of the buttress, the gut safety of knowing he could no longer be hit.

And then concrete, earth, safety, all crumbled away. He broke out in a sweat. As he realised that the man had been here, waiting for him, all the time. Expecting him. He'd seen the Audi in the street, perhaps seen Martin earlier, much earlier, running through the storm of headlights in Akademias Street.

The man in the dark expensive suit, who moved lightly, carefully . . . And even now moving round to take him from the side, around the buttress.

He stared out at the shadows, trying to make them real, trying to make one of them flesh and blood, quiet breathing flesh and blood, moving in to kill him . . . But he couldn't. Instead, in his fear, a strange dream began to assemble.

It began with the doll, the cheap doll staring up at him from the courtyard not three yards away . . . Then the ventilators, the rows of glowing plastic mushrooms . . . Farther away the rocking chair standing on top of a heap of white sand . . . And all around the buildings with square yellow windows, a thirties stage set.

A dream . . . Because suddenly even in the hardness of concrete where he lay, suddenly there was a click, the sound of a motor. And a black weight, huge, the size of a cabin trunk, coming straight down at him between rails.

No. Not a dream . . . The rails were real. He could touch them . . . Rails, yes, oiled gleaming rails. And the strange buffer arrangement that he'd seen before, with its coiled springs, its thick greased bar.

The black weight came down, right down, close to him, and bounced against the buffer. There was another click. The motor stopped.

Then what? What the noise now? From far away? . . . Gates? . . . Yes, gates. Lift gates. First one opening, then the other.

Lift gates. A lift . . . And the weight was its counter-weight, outside the building. Coming down when the lift went up, and going up when it . . .

. . . New sounds now. The lift gates closing. One, then the other. Again the click.

. . . And as the counterweight started upwards, he grabbed it, locked his arms round the cable, held on.

A shot smacked into the wall just below him. There were running feet behind him. Another shot, wide . . . And then the angle was too narrow, he was rising between the gleaming rails, up into the night.

He didn't look down. He didn't look to one side or the other. He only had one thought . . . That the lift itself had to go right down to the basement garage. Or else he was going to be hanging on the outside of the building, halfway up it.

The sound of the motor, the winding gear on the roof, came nearer. He shut his eyes, unable to look.

And then he heard the click, felt the sudden motion of buffers. The lift was in the basement, he was up at the top.

Still he didn't look down. He looked only at the parapet that was four feet above him. At the handhold on the

149

buffers, the foothold on the counterweight, that would get him up there.

He gripped oil, old congealed oil. His hand slipped. He swung one-handed, one-footed over space . . . But he swung back, scrabbled at the first object he felt, one of the cables. It was frayed. It hurt, stung him into calm. He hung there for a moment, panting. Then he got a higher foothold and hauled himself up onto the parapet, the roof.

It was a moment before he could move. Before he could look up and see the lift-house above him, breaking the sky-line. It was reached by a flight of railed steps, and it had a door. He went up there. The door was locked, and he pressed his ear against it, listening.

Far below he could hear the sound of lift gates opening, staying open. Then the sound of feet running up steps . . . The man, boxing clever. Immobilising the lift and taking the stairs.

Martin looked round. The next apartment block was joined to this one, with just a spiked fence separating the two. And on the next building there was another lift-house, another door.

He ran, hauled his way carefully over the spikes, and ran on. But the door he came to was locked . . . And the one on the next building, and the next.

It became a dream again. But not the same dream as before. Now as if he were running through other people's dreams. Because he was high up, on catwalks and ventilator shafts, running in darkness. And there were people below, in penthouse apartments, thinking they were unobserved.

There was the party, the laughing shouting crowd. And away in the kitchen, the girl on her own. She was opening and closing the fridge door, its light was falling across her, and she was crying. There was the terrace with the husband and the wife sitting far apart from one another. He holding a dog up by its forepaws, talking to it, and with every honeyed word kicking it in the stomach.

150

Martin ran on. And then the dream became his again, his alone, his nightmare. Because the man was behind him again, far back, but still behind him . . . And ahead of him, the roofs ended. There were lights, moving headlights far below. A side street, with no way round.

Dreamlike he reached out for a thick bunch of cables, phone cables that went across it, supported by a heavy metal hawser. Dreamlike he started swinging himself over.

He was halfway across when a shot passed him. And as he pulled himself onto the far roof, another shot. He got up. The roof was sloping. Steep. His foot slipped as he tried to edge away. And he stood there, unable to move.

On the other roof the man fired again. It was a pistol. He held it how the police held it in movies, two-handed. The shots were close. And all Martin could do was sway, feet slipping, from side to side.

The man re-loaded. He fired again, twice more. Then he slid the pistol back into his shoulder holster, clipped it there.

Martin waited. The man came quickly, his body coiled around the cables. Three-quarters of the way over he changed position. He looped one arm over the cables and gripped the wrist of his other hand so that it was never far from his holster. And he came on. There were lines, hard taut lines on his face, but they were of concentration.

The gun came out. A shot whistled close to Martin's side. And Martin suddenly saw he could do it, could shoot him either from the cables or climb, gun in hand, onto the roof.

The roof. It was of some black tar paint, slippery. On either side of it there were large ventilator shafts going up towards the crest. But then, by the right-hand shaft, Martin noticed treads, wooden treads that went up like a ladder.

He squatted down. On hands and knees he edged his way towards the treads, got to them, climbed them, reached the crest.

'THE HELL, YOU SAY! HE'S GOT A GUN!'

. . . Dream?

151

The dream now?

Jake Mallows?

Jake Mallows?

Mallows, all-American film star, thirty feet from nostril to nostril, in dirty battle fatigues, with a Thompson machine gun.

Martin threw himself flat.

And suddenly . . . suddenly realised he'd seen the picture before.

Hell At Camp Nine. Paramount. 1958.

The widening beam of light was there, from the projection-box somewhere below him. The huge screen was there, perhaps a hundred yards away, with just the front rows of the audience visible . . . A rooftop cinema. One of the flickering screens he'd seen with Lela that night, from the Lykavettos restaurant. The Athens cinemas that she'd told him moved bodily up onto their own rooftops, in the summer heat.

He thought for a moment, realised why the soundtrack had hit him so suddenly . . . The steeply sloping roof, the ventilator shafts on either side of it, funnelling the sound.

. . . And the man had to come up the same way, climbing those wooden treads.

Quickly Martin looked round him. He crawled towards one of the ventilator shafts. It was fastened to the roof by lengths of girder. One of them, a metal bar three feet long, was loose. He wrenched it free. Then he hauled himself back to the roof-crest again, stopped just below the top, keeping as much of himself as he could in the ventilator's shadow.

The man appeared, crouching.

'FOR CHRISSAKES!' Huge Jake Mallows, swinging the Thompson machine gun.

The man threw himself down, pistol forward and out.

Martin grunted, swung savagely with the bar.

The pistol skipped, bounced down the roof to land against the parapet below.

Martin started after it, feeling his way down the girders of the shaft.

But even with his pain, his dreadful pain, the man was quicker, sliding, rolling.

To land heavily against the brickwork. Six feet from the pistol.

Martin got to it, a Lüger, he knew it only from the movies.

Movies. All around them from that huge exploding screen was the whine, the ricochet, the rimshot snare of American war.

And the man, facing Martin, crouching. Then sliding his hand forward along the parapet, edging forward.

Martin backed. He glanced quickly at the pistol, saw it was cocked, saw the safety catch was on. But he knew nothing more, nothing at all. Rifles he'd fired, many sorts of rifles. But . . .

The man came on.

Martin raised the pistol.

All hell on the screen. All-dancing-jerking, gun-hosepiping hell. Mallows roaring, firing from the hip.

And Martin with no idea, none. Except that a pistol kicked. He aimed low.

Shot low.

Onscreen, rows of Japanese fell cleanly, arms raised, without a mark.

The man cracked over, hit his head. From his groin a dark spreading stain.

But still he came on. Surprise, yes, surprise on his face.

Martin fired again. Higher, trying, Jesus, trying to finish it . . . Trying *what*? The gun shaking in his hand, all balance gone.

White bone showed on the man's shoulder.

He slumped. Or rather his body slumped. His face was still forward, watching Martin, his eyes never leaving him.

It lasted, what, thirty seconds? While Jake Mallows mowed down man after man.

Then, gradually, silence on the screen. The American flag. Mallows under it. Sweat from a spray-bottle, and soul-searching as deep as an agent's reader.

'AIN'T BUT ONE THING TO DO IN THIS MAN'S ARMY.'

'You bastard, Raikes,' the man said.

'GET DRUNKER'N A HORSES'S ASS.'

'Bastard, Raikes. You're a marksman, a goddam marks-man.'

The two scenes swirled, mixed in Martin's mind. Dimly he understood that the man thought he'd shot for those two wounds, those two pumping wounds, on purpose.

Onscreen there was a fade-out to darkness. Then a fade-in. Sunlight, Hula girls, Hawaiian guitars . . . It was easy to shut those out.

But not easy, as Martin turned, to shut out the way the man sat, wet-fingered, clutching his groin. And the chips of white bone on his shoulder.

'Bastard, Raikes. I got half an hour. Maybe half an hour. I know that.'

'What?'

'And I knew it was you too. Knew you'd work your way up from Yarvis, Fotcheion, those nothings. Work your way up to where it mattered . . . I said you'd do it. But nobody else could see it that way.'

Work your way up. To where it mattered . . . Martin saw past the wounds then, to the expensive suit, shirt, tie. He saw the only thing that was creased and used about the man, the soft-leather holster under his arm.

To where it mattered . . . The man moved then, reached into his pocket. He got something out, threw it down onto the stonework in front of Martin. A set of keys.

Then his hand clutched his groin again. 'A deal,' he said.

'Deal?'

'Yeah. You get to my apartment. You get there in three minutes. You get a number from a certain book, and you

154

ring. A doc. He speaks English. You tell him it's bad, he has to be quick.'

'*Me?* Me do that? But . . .?'

'A deal,' the man repeated. 'In that certain book there's another phone-number, an address. The guy you want.'

'What?' Suddenly Martin's mind cleared. 'Elegesis? You mean him?'

'That's it. Only his name ain't that. It's Stefanides. Yorgo Stefanides.'

Martin looked down at the keys. 'How do I know you're telling the truth?' he asked then.

And just for a moment the man took his hands away from his groin. Martin saw the pump there, the slow dark pump.

He turned away. Onscreen there was a broad strip of white sand, the blue Pacific, palm trees . . . peace . . . And Jake Mallows looking at it all from the bonnet of a jeep.

'SONOFABITCH,' he said. 'SONOFABITCH.'

29

One of the keys opened the lift door in the garage basement. Another fitted Apartment 11, on the fifth floor. Martin went in.

It was empty. And something else too that he hadn't expected. It was rich, strangely English rich. There were polished parquet floors, with good rugs and carpets. Heavy furniture stood between large brocade lampshades, and on the walls there were leather-bound books, new, never handled.

Martin went past sitting room, dining room, and bedroom, and came to the door beyond. The office, the man had called it. Inside there were more shelves, and a large carved desk with a typewriter on it. Martin bent down. He put one hand on each side of the carved capital between desk-top and drawers, as he'd been told, and pulled. A narrow hidden drawer came into view. And inside it, the phone book.

S . . .
Yorgos Stefanides.
Kokkinos Pyrgos.
Neos Paradisos.
Glyfada.
73-828-604.
. . . He tore the page out.

Then he found the other page, the one with the English-speaking doctor's number on it. And he hesitated. For some time he looked idly down at the desk-top. At the typewriter, an electric machine, the expensive golf-ball type. At the spare golf-balls, wrapped in polythene in a small case, some with English characters, some with Greek. He picked one of them up, threw it in the air, caught it, threw it again.

156

Then he thought of the seconds passing, and of that dark pumping stain in the man's groin.

He phoned the doctor.

Lela was waiting, her face pale and nervous, behind the wheel of the Audi.

She gripped his arm, held on. 'What happened? Where've you been?' she asked.

'Don't worry about that now, it's over. It's where we're going on to.' He showed her the paper.

'Stefanides?' Her mouth opened. 'Yorgos Stefanides?'

'You know him?'

'I've heard of him. Everybody's heard of him. He's big ... Shipbuilding, shipping, property development.'

'And d'you know what he looks like?'

'Well, he's in the paper, on newsreels.'

'Right. Then you can point him out.' He showed her the address below the man's name.

'But, Martin,' she was alarmed, '*Neos Paradisos*. You don't understand. It's ...'

'... It's what? New Paradise, isn't that what it means?'

'Yes, but ...'

'There's no time,' he said.

And there wasn't. It was now nearly half-past twelve.

Just nine-and-a-half hours to go.

30

They were out past the airport along the coast. The sound of planes was distant, a screeching in the darkness. But where they stood there was silence, hills sloping down to the sea in folds of scrub and gorse. There were roads too, pale in the moonlight, linking the lights of distant villas. And lower, by the sea's edge, a line where scrub and gorse ended, where there were rocks, bone-white as they met the water. Except for one narrow bay. There were tall trees down there, the deep shadows of a wood, and yet hanging over it an aura of bright light.

Martin and Lela walked slowly down the hillside. When they reached the wood they found to their amazement that the trees had wire stays to keep them upright. Transplanted trees, growing on transplanted soil. And, even more strangely, on certain trunks they found electric power points, on others the gleam of telephones.

The light ahead grew bright now, very bright. As they edged forward, they came to a track running towards a high ornamental wall. It ended by a gate that was ornamental too. But all its wrought iron couldn't conceal the fact that it was massive, with massive backstops set in concrete. To one side there was a gatehouse with thin slits for windows. There were dark uniformed men standing there, keeping discreetly back in the shadows. And the shadows were hard. From this close distance the lights were blinding, as bright as day.

Martin turned. He led Lela away from the gatehouse, parallel to the wall. Except that it wasn't just a wall now. Between it and the trees were two wire fences, one on each side of a metalled road. And on the outer fence there were notices. In three languages they said that all normal services, police, fire, and ambulance, stopped beyond this point.

Without thinking Martin brushed his arm against the fence. And he felt an electric shock, not a strong one, perhaps no more than that of a cattle wire. But the inner fence, he guessed as he looked at it, would carry a higher voltage. He looked on, at the strip of clear ground between it and the wall . . . Too clear. There wasn't a trace of litter, not a stone larger than a foot in diameter, not a weed that grew . . . And the lights. It was too brightly lit . . . Then he saw them, high up on the wall, the glass eyes, convex, like fish-eyes. The wide-angle lenses of a closed-circuit system.

He took Lela on through the shadows of that strange artificial forest. They moved always in the same direction, towards the sound of the sea. Because the high wall had to end, had to, at the water's edge.

And it did. But there was a second guardhouse, a second building with slit windows built down upon the white rocks. And beyond . . . In the water a line of light. Bright spotlights were set into the bottom of the bay, crossing its narrow opening to the guardhouse on the far side.

New Paradise.

They were on higher ground now, the rocky outcrop right at the mouth of the bay, and they could look back and see it all. The ring of bright light, on the land and in the water. Light that was hidden from the hillside by the man-made forest . . . And inside it the large shadowy villas, maybe a dozen of them set in a semicircle, each with its steps down to a private beach.

And it shouldn't have come as a surprise. Lela had told him about it during the car ride from Athens. She'd talked of cabinet ministers, industrialists, tycoons. Of the ever growing fear of kidnap, of assassination.

. . . And Halkis too. Something he'd said that night in the car. *Assassination, it's an industry nowadays, Martin, there are buildings going up . . .*

159

Buildings going up. Martin wondered how many villages there were like this around the Mediterranean. Shoreside villages, without a fishing boat in sight. Where the fish, the fruit and vegetables came in refrigerated trucks. Where the police force outnumbered the residents, and where the barking came from dogs that hunted men. The new village of the rich. The fortress.

'That's his house,' Lela said then, 'Stefanides'.'

'That one? There on the right?' He followed her pointing finger. 'How . . .? How d'you know?'

'*Kokkinos Pyrgos*, red tower,' she said. 'D'you see it? The tower? There, floodlit above the house?'

'Yes.'

'And *Kokkinos Pyrgos* is the name of a village too, in Southern Crete,' she went on. 'Stefanides comes from there.'

He looked across the water at the red tower, old, perhaps transported stone by stone from Crete. Then he looked at the house below, the long crinkle-tiled roof, the terrace, and the steps leading down from the terrace to the narrow white crescent of a beach.

'What are you going to do?' Lela asked.

'Kill him.'

And she was shocked by his voice, the change in it. 'You mean that, don't you?'

'Yes. I kill him before he kills my children. It's as simple as that.'

She shivered. 'But you can't reach him. Well, you can't, can you?'

He didn't answer.

'And maybe it's better you can't. Because it wouldn't help. All it'd mean is you'd be deeper in. You'd be wanted for two murders, Grivela's and his.'

He sat down on the rocks. The ring of lights faced him over the water, unwinking, steady.

'You've got to understand how completely they've set you up,' Lela said. 'Look. Just look at that place over there. That's money. They're rich Greeks, and that means some of the richest men in the world . . . Money . . . They built an entire film company, Elpart Productions, around you. You, one man . . . I know, because I was there, remember, working for them. And I was there too when that film company was destroyed. Every last paper, every schedule, crossplot, script. Destroyed. Because the whole thing only had to last two days . . . That's money.'

He stared on at the lights. A breeze crossed the water, dragging their reflections out into moving lines . . . Then suddenly he stiffened. He turned round towards Lela. He stared at her. 'Say that again.'

'What?'

'The last bit. That last thing you said.'

'What? Something about money?'

'No. Before that.'

'I don't know . . . Papers being destroyed, was that it? Every schedule, every crossplot, every script.'

Every script.

He didn't know when it first came to him . . . the picture of a restaurant, of oilcloth tables, a metal jug of wine. The shade of an awning and the hard sun of midday . . . The restaurant he'd gone to from the office that day, with the scripts. Six scripts, in two plain envelopes.

And left one envelope behind.

When? A week ago?

It wasn't until he'd worked it out, gone over everything that had happened to him, that he realised it was only four days.

Four days.

The scripts could still be there.

Proof. The first proof that he'd come to Athens why he said he had, to work on a TV series. He couldn't let the thought go.

Until something else came to him . . . In the envelope with the scripts there'd been paper, Elpart Productions paper he'd taken with him to make notes.

Elpart Productions paper.

. . . How completely they've set you up . . .

Suddenly it came to him that he could turn it around. He could set them up.

The man who mattered, Stefanides.

It took a long time to work it out.

Yarvis came into it, something Yarvis had said earlier this evening. About left-luggage lockers. How he'd been paid.

Money came into it, the assassin's $25,000 he'd found in Yarvis' garage.

Then, the gunman's apartment, up on the hill in Athens. The room at the end of its corridor, the office.

. . . Lela, who'd worked as Production Secretary for Elpart.

And then, as he looked once again at the ring of lights, something else came into it too . . . That however big Stefanides might be, there were still people higher up. The people in North Europe who'd arranged the assassination.

Assassination . . . The final idea. The idea that tied everything else up. And linked it to his children, sleeping unharmed in that house in England. Unharmed till 10 o'clock tomorrow morning.

And the thing that could keep them unharmed. The thing he could do. The one weapon he had.

The long range rifle.

He looked across at the tiny crescent of beach that was, what, maybe a quarter of a mile, maybe a third of a mile away?

It wasn't possible.

But he got up, pulled Lela to her feet.

The car was where they'd left it, parked just off the main road at the top of the hill.

The red Michelin Guide was in its boot. He got it out, found the map insert of Glyfada, the bay where they were.

. . . The village, the fortress village of the millionaires, wasn't marked on it, he hadn't expected it to be. But the

162

shape of the land was there. The rocky point where Lela and he had sat, and that narrow crescent of beach.

With a small length of wire he found the distance between them, and measured it on the scale below.

600 metres.

It wasn't possible. No professional assassin in the world would try a shot over 200 metres, 250 at the most. He was sure of that.

But he wouldn't allow himself to think of it. All he concentrated on was a day at Bisley years ago, the best shooting he'd ever done in his life. It hadn't been at Stickledown, the 1,000 yards range, but at Century . . . 600 yards . . . the same range as now.

It had been the day he'd borrowed a rich man's rifle, the Number Four with the sort of barrel that always seemed to come rich men's way . . . And it had been a 'possible', 2 sighters followed by 10 straight bulls.

But the sort of 'possible' you made once in a lifetime . . . 8 of those bulls had been within a circle of 7 inches.

Rich man's rifle . . . He looked down now at the padded slipcover in the car boot. One thing, and one thing only was on his side. This was a rich man's rifle, there was no doubt about that.

31

It was two a.m.

Martin looked out from the parked Audi at the row of oilcloth tables, the restaurant that was near Antonadis Street. It was still open, just as Lela had said it would be. There were still red-faced tourists dancing and clapping to a *bouzouki* band.

He watched them through the windscreen, watched Lela talking to a group of waiters beyond.

Then one of the waiters reached behind a counter and handed her a large plain envelope.

Martin ripped it open as soon as she got back into the car.

'THE STRIKER'   Episode 1
FADE IN TO:
1   GREEK FISHING HARBOR. EXT. DAY.
A small harbor, backed by white store-fronts, discos, a boutique or two. It's noon, the water bounces back the sun . . .

And Elpart Productions headed paper. Maybe twenty sheets of it.

He drove slowly now, being careful, not sure if he trusted what Elegesis had said in his phone-call . . . or rather what Stefanides had said . . . that the police patrols had been called off. But it seemed true enough. There were no flashing lights, no sirens.

They returned to the street high on Lykavettos Hill, the street of the gunman's apartment. Martin got out, he opened the boot and took out the parcel containing $25,000 in notes. Then he led Lela along the pavement, and down the sloping ramp to the underground garage.

They went up in the lift to the apartment on the fifth floor. And Martin's movements were confident now. He wasn't worried about the gunman, not after those two terrible wounds on the cinema roof, the doctor he'd called, the surgery that was going to be somewhere in the back-streets.

And the rooms of the apartment were empty, just as he'd seen them before. He took Lela on past the row of doors to the office, where the desk was, and the electric golf-ball typewriter.

He sat her down at the desk. He got the Elpart headed paper from the envelope and inserted a sheet into the machine. Then he stared at the whiteness of the paper, his eyes half-closed, and thought.

'We'll get the words right first,' he said. 'And we can do that, can't we, between us? . . . I mean, you did the typing in the first place? You were the Production Secretary with the English degree?'

She nodded.

'Right . . . Pro-Forma Contract,' he began.

ELPART PRODUCTIONS INC.

3001 La Jolla Ave.,	Antonidas 14,
Los Angeles,	Athens,
Calif.	Greece.

Pro-Forma Contract.

LETTER OF AGREEMENT between ....
(hereinafter known as the Company) and ....
(hereinafter known as The Technician), dated this
.... (day), of .... (month), 197......

It took them an hour to work out the five clauses, the one that was to do with the exclusive rights to his work, the one that was to do with his fifty-per-cent credit, the one that was the standard Union Agreement . . . Not that they were exactly right. The fine print, the wheretofores and where-ases were only approximate. But they were near enough.

It took Lela another ten minutes to type it out again, but as a copy this time, a carbon copy.

Then she changed the golf-ball on the machine for one with a different type-face. And she went back over the contract for a third and last time, typing in the names and dates.

Finally she reached out for a ballpoint pen. She practised with it for some time on a scribble pad. Then signed Elegesis' name.

And Martin signed his.

After that it was easier. They were all letters. Letters he knew well.

ELPART PRODUCTIONS INC.

3001 La Jolla Ave.,   Antonadis 14,
Los Angeles,   Athens,
Calif.   Greece.

July 5, 1978.

Dear Mr Raikes,

Your name has been recommended me by British director Dan Leater. He is at present engaged by my Company, Elpart Productions, on a 13-part TV Series, 'The Striker', to be made in Greece.

Filming starts in Athens, end July. Dan tells me your work is the best. And I write to ask now if you'd like to join our team as Supervising Cutter/Second Unit Director on the Series. It will be a long haul. We are cutting in Athens, processing there, and pre- and post-production will take the best part of a year.

If you can take such a large chunk out of your life, and if you're free, why not call at the London Hilton, Monday, July 17? My representative will be there at twelve noon, and will be glad to lunch you and talk terms.

Hoping to see a great deal more of you in the future.

Cordially,

Dimitri Elegesis

ELPART PRODUCTIONS INC.

3001 La Jolla Ave.,   Antonadis 14,
Los Angeles,   Athens,
Calif.   Greece.

July 19, 1978.

Dear Mr Raikes,

As of last Monday's lunch with my representative, Mr Yanni Houmousiades, I'm happy to confirm $1,000 a week as Supervising Cutter, rising to $2,000 a week for any time spent directing Second Unit.

Glad to have you on the team. Will be in touch soonest, by the end of the week anyway.

Cordially,

Dimitri Elegesis

ELPART PRODUCTIONS INC.

3001 La Jolla Ave.,   Antonadis 14,
Los Angeles,   Athens,
Calif.   Greece.

July 22, 1978.

Dear Mr Raikes,

Re *your appointment as Supervising Cutter/Second Unit Director on 'The Striker' Series. A booking has been made for you on London–Athens Flight BE 076, July 25. Also a booking at the Ariadne Hotel, Athens, for the same night.*

I look forward to meeting you here at the Production Offices, Antonadis 14, on July 26. A car will call at your hotel at 9.30 a.m.

Cordially,

Dimitri Elegesis

But the fourth letter, the last, was more difficult. Martin thought for some time. And just before he began dictating, he remembered suddenly that this one couldn't be on Elpart paper, nor could it be a carbon copy. 'Oh, and make a few typing mistakes as well,' he said. 'This wasn't written by a secretary, nor by some clever Greek pretending to be a film producer. This was written by the man himself.'

'Him?' Lela's mouth opened. 'You mean, Stefanides?'

'That's right. Date it a couple of days ago, say, July 29. And begin it, Dear Mr ... Mr Sorenson.'

'Sorenson?'

'Sorenson, Grüning, Armitage,' he said. 'Any North European name will do.'

July 29, 1978.

Dear Mr Sorenson,

Your $25,000 arrived yesterday. You'll agree it was a fair price to pay for a sample, just a small sample. And I hope you'll agree too that the enclosed package, (scripts, letters, a contract), will stand the asking price of $250,000. There is just one more package to follow this, at the same price. And as I'm sure you'll understand, this will bring my fee up to the figure I originally quoted so long ago.

I've learned a couple of movie terms in the last few months. And there's one maybe you should remember. Post-production. The picture isn't finished at the end of shooting. You always have to allow for post-production in the budget.

> *Cordially as ever,*
>
> S.

'I don't understand,' Lela said.

'What does it look like?' Martin asked her. 'I mean, what would it look like if you were a policeman and you found it? In a package? Together with the other letters, contract, and scripts? . . . If you were a policeman, say, who had some idea that S meant Stefanides? *And* if you found, somewhere else, $25,000 that could also be traced back to Stefanides?'

She nodded slowly, working it out. 'That Stefanides was heavily involved in the assassination, perhaps running the Greek end of it,' she said.

'And?'

'That he was blackmailing someone, someone outside Greece who was paying him. A man called Sorenson.'

'That's it,' he told her, 'I got the idea from Yarvis. D'you remember, back at his house, earlier on? Yarvis kept saying this job was *unusual*. So unusual he was going to stay where he wasn't meant to be and keep his eyes open. He said there was money in it.'

'And now? The same thing?'

'On a much higher level,' he said. 'Stefanides working his way towards real money, half a million dollars. And that stands up. If the assassination was financed outside Greece, as they keep telling us. Northern European money.'

'And you mean,' Lela hesitated, 'you mean, Stefanides didn't destroy all the proof of Elpart Productions? He kept some back? To use it?'

'His file copies.' Martin nodded. 'You remember I got you to type everything but the last letter in carbon?'

She was silent. 'It could work, just about work,' she said then. 'But how will they be found? These letters? This package?'

'In a left-luggage locker. I got that idea from Yarvis too. The way he was paid, the way he handed over the keys of the Audi.'

'And the money? How will that be found?'

'I don't know. I haven't thought about that yet.'

'But $25,000? It's nothing to a man like Stefanides. Well, is it?'

'It's a start, a sample. You remember he said just that in his letter.' He shrugged. 'And there's one thing about money, isn't there? It's always believed . . . $25,000 is a lot to a policeman.'

'But the rest of it,' she insisted. 'The other payment? $250,000?'

Martin waited, let the silence hang. 'A quarter of a million?' he said then. 'They weren't going to pay that, were

169

they? Not when they had another answer? A man who'd worked for them once before?'

She didn't understand.

'You remember that rocky point where we were sitting opposite Stefanides' villa?' he asked. 'Well, tomorrow morning a gun's going to be found on those rocks there, an assassin's rifle, and a couple of empty cartridges.'

Her eyes clouded. He knew she was no longer seeing him, but that distance, that great gap of water between rocks and beach. 'No,' she said. 'It can't be done.'

He saw the distance then, and he knew she was right, but he didn't let it show. 'Once,' he said, 'over the same range at Bisley, 600 yards, I did something just like it. It's the sort of thing you can do, even the best shots say they can do, just once, like the four minute mile.'

'Once,' she repeated. 'Just once.' And slowly she shook her head.

He pointed at the letters and the contract they'd written. 'Look,' he said, 'these things can clear me, get me clear . . . But if I don't want my children killed tomorrow, I have to get that shot in. Have to. Make no mistake about that.'

He thought about the shot then. He opened the Michelin Guide at the map insert of Glyfada, looked for some time at the narrow crescent beach, at the rocky promontory. And then back, behind the promontory, along the coast. There were beaches there, hotel and public beaches as far as he could see, maybe half a mile away.

Beaches.

He went into the gunman's bedroom. In a drawer he found a pair of bathing trunks. And later, in the kitchen, he found a waterproof bag, a polythene sandwich bag, and an elastic band.

Lela was still sitting exactly as he'd left her, by the office desk, her face still pressed against the knuckles of one hand.

And he saw the scar, that red line on her wrist where she'd slashed at it with the razor.

And suddenly he remembered.

170

The police will find you, she'd said. *They'll find out what you know, and I'll be killed.*

The police who'd already known about the assassination before it happened. They'd let it happen.

You've got to think in a bigger way, she'd said, *beyond the way you'd normally think, anyone would.*

And the voice on the phone this evening. *The girl's dead. Every time you look at her, remember that.*

He reached down and touched her shoulder. 'There'll be a way,' he said, 'a place we can get you to. It's only a question of finding it.'

She shook her head.

But in the end they found it, a place of sorts.

The British Embassy . . . The one organisation in the country that wanted Martin Raikes, misfit, *and* British subject, cleared.

'We go there, and not to the police,' Martin told her. 'Or rather *you* go there. *You* be the one who clears me. You go tomorrow, after ten in the morning, and you offer to do a deal.'

'A deal?'

'Asylum, somewhere out of the country . . . as against information you've got.'

'What information?'

'A key. A key to a left luggage locker with certain documents inside.' He pointed to the letters and contract. '*And* the whereabouts of a parcel containing $25,000 . . . I'm not sure how we arrange that last bit yet, but it has to be something like . . . Yes, look, this could be it . . .' He bent over her. '. . . You worked for Stefanides during the assassination, and you're still working for him. What you're doing at the moment is going between him and a man called Sorenson, carrying letters and parcels . . . And you're frightened. It's getting too big. Stefanides is frightened too. He's heard a rumour the assassin's back in the country . . .'

She saw it was possible, just about possible. But for some

171

reason it made no difference to her. Her cheek was still pressed tight against her knuckles, and she looked away from him, past the corner of the desk.

Dawn light came in through the window. Her face was in shadow. 'Five years,' she said. 'Most of them last five years.'

'Who?'

'The people who ask for asylum. I've seen it before . . . They go to America mostly, because there are so many immigrants there. They're set up in a small apartment, given a small salary. But what they're not allowed to do is talk Greek any more, talk to Greeks. It's too risky . . . So, after five years they come back. And then there's a car accident, or maybe just an unexplained death.'

'No,' Martin said. 'You'll manage it. You'll stay there. You'll get a good job in the States, meet some good man. You'll see.'

But she shook her head. 'It'll start this morning when I walk into the Embassy,' she said. 'The smell there. You can't know what it's like because you're used to it . . . But to me, the smell of Virginia tobacco. The smell of people who eat too much meat, the wrong foods. The smell of paperwork, of power. And that strongest of all smells, the most hateful – deodorisers . . . For me it'll start this morning, the cage.'

She turned and looked out at the sky, the whiteness that was just coming into it, the shiver that was there, the life.

He took her into the bedroom. He laid her on the bed and loved her with his hands, just his hands, as he'd done before. Stroking the hollows of her neck, her back, and her shoulders. But it was no use now. Because he saw the darkness of her again, under her arms, the slight fur behind her jaw, the very fine dark hairs between her breasts . . . And against her his hands, large, freckled, pale.

And it was as if she saw them too. As if for her they were the first of many pale hands, and she had already left this city. She lay quite still, but with her eyes open, every muscle, every wire within her taut.

He stroked her as the dawn light grew, as the sounds of the day began. But then suddenly it was six o'clock, and he knew he could no longer stay. He kissed the back of her neck and stood up. But she didn't turn round, didn't look at him.

And he left.

32

It was nearly seven o'clock.

There were just over three hours to go.

He was driving on the coast road again, but now a long way past the airport, and past Glyfada where the millionaires' village was.

He slowed, drew off the road, and parked.

Anavyssos, the name of the bay was there on the Michelin map. And the huge square shapes were there too . . . the salt pans.

They lay in front of him and to his left, each like a man-made lake, brilliant white or mud-coloured, according to its stage of evaporation. There were railway tracks running between them, buckled and corroded, and every now and then an abandoned tipper truck. Beyond in the distance tall pointed heaps rose up, slagheaps except that they were dazzling white, of salt. It was a strange white landscape where not a figure stirred.

He went to the boot of the car, took off his jacket and put on the overalls. The overalls that had thick elbow pads sewn into the sleeves, smelling of the assassin's sweat. He picked up the man's duffel-bag, emptied it of its stale sandwiches and thermos, and then filled it with rocks from the roadside. Finally he picked up the slip-cover that contained the gun.

He walked past the first salt pan. It took him a long time, and then he went down the steeply sloping wall of the second. The sunlight left him. It formed a bluish-white line on the distant wall to his left, and he was walking in a strange world, like snow. The sound was like snow too, the crunch-crunch of his footsteps. They made a straight line behind him until he stopped, put down the duffel-bag again, and rested the gun on it.

He looked around him until he saw what he wanted. Away to his right in the corner of the salt pan were the sluice-gates that let seawater in. They were made up of boards, about four feet by four, and there were wooden props to keep them in place. He went over and took hold of two of them, and an armful of wooden props. Then he returned to the gun.

He left both the boards and the props by it, and started pacing diagonally out across the huge salt pan. He kept in a straight line by glancing back at his footsteps behind him. And he paced as exactly as he did every summer on the lawn at home, marking out Simon's cricket pitch. He counted two hundred paces, stopped, and made a wide mark. He counted another four hundred on after that, and made a second mark.

Then he set up the boards, one after the other, on the marks. He set them up against the props, which he dug as deeply into the salt as he could.

He returned to where he'd started. He took the stone-filled duffel-bag and positioned it firmly as a barrel-rest. Then he lay down behind it, the rifle still in its slip-cover to protect it from the salt. He unbuttoned the pocket on the outside of the cover, and took out a charger. Five rounds of Raufoss Match ammunition.

He slid the gun out, laid it carefully on top of the slip-cover, and pressed the five rounds home into the breech. And only then did he look at the sight adjustments below the fat telescope . . . He breathed out a sigh of relief. Parker Hale's. That solid English gleam to the metal. That exactly fitting Scale Plate between the single engraved arrow on one side, and the Vernier on the other.

And a second sigh of relief when he found that the elevation was set at 1 inch above 200 yards. Because the assassin had fired at around 225 yards back in that Athens street. And now Martin knew that the rifle had been zeroed as he

would have zeroed it himself, at an elevation of 200 . . .
And the rest, he knew that too. That the proper zeroing
target had been used, at the proper range of exactly 71 feet
7 inches.

He felt good then as he pressed himself down into the
salt, found his position. He fitted his left arm through the
loop of the sling, tightened it high on his left arm above
the elbow pad, and lowered the gun until the back of his
left hand was on the duffel-bag.

200 yards, it leapt at him. 200 yards had always been
easy, had always felt as though he could reach out and
touch the target with his finger . . . At 200, after coming
back from 600 or 1,000 his only problem had been to *make*
it difficult, to get his shots right into the centre of that
massive bull, and therefore avoid the error.

. . . And now 200 yards through a 'scope, where at Bisley
'scopes were only allowed at ranges of 1,000 or over . . .
200 yards felt as though he could touch the target with his
nose.

He raised his head, checked that the wind-gauge was at
zero, clicked off the safety catch, and found his position
again. The hairlines of the 'scope crossed in the centre of
the wooden sluice-gate. There was a slight lurching, a slight
pumping in his head. That was normal, and he waited for
it to subside. He took the two shallow breaths, and then the
slightly deeper one.

And found what he'd always been able to find. That
world. Inside his head. The tube that seemed to go away
through the tube of the 'scope, through the air, to the
centre of the target. The tube, the vacuum, that had nothing special about it, was just something he could do. The
silence of it, a loneliness even. But that masculine loneliness
of precision, of fastening onto just the one thing.

Which was now, as it always had been, that moment.
The moment his breath was steady, not too tight. The
moment his right hand locked the position in, without a
question of doubt. And the moment, as with any gun of

176

course, of metal . . . First pressure taken on the trigger. And then feeling that edge, that *last* edge of the metal rib, before it released the sear.

He fired once. He fired twice. And he felt good. There was the slight taste of blood in his mouth, the cut inside his lip that would later become a bruise. Because he'd always fired with his cheek pressed against his thumb, closer than other people, far closer. But he'd found that this way he could use the strength of his arm and not his hand. And all right, he'd walked around Bisley with a bruised right cheek, but he'd also walked round with a good-looking score book and prize money in the bank.

And now . . . now he didn't even have to look. At the two shots, maybe $2\frac{1}{2}$ inches apart, in the centre of the wooden sluice gate.

He turned his attention to the other one, the far one at 600 yards. He lowered the rifle and looked at the sight adjustment again . . . 200 to 500, up 11 inches . . . 200 to 600, up 16 inches . . . The figures were still printed somewhere inside his memory. And now he turned the milled elevation knob clockwise through 16 inches, or 32 clicks.

Which was why he was here. To set the elevation for 600 yards. To see whether with this particular rifle it was + 16 inches, + 17 inches, or + $14\frac{1}{2}$ inches. It varied from gun to gun. And at this range, at 600 yards, 3 inches of wrong elevation could throw him two feet off target.

He fired again, three shots now, at + 16 inches. Three very, very careful shots.

And he could just see them, the holes and the splinter marks, through the 'scope. They were more spread, perhaps nine inches between the three. They were to the right, almost on the edge of the wooden board . . . But that was wind . . . And there was no way of reading the wind, however slight it might be, down here in the salt-pan.

But the shots were also high, nearly two feet high.

High Velocity rounds. Match Rifle rounds. Of course.

He came down 3 inches on the elevation, and fired again,

risking three more rounds of his remaining total of ten. And he took a long time over those shots. For the second one even breaking the aim and starting again from the beginning.

They were in the centre of the sluice-gate, as far as elevation went, but the wind was still taking him out to the right.

The wind . . .

He stood up and slipped the rifle back into its cover. He told himself it all felt good, the grouping of the barrel, the trigger pressure, even the length of stock he was used to. A rich man's rifle, all right.

But the wind . . .

And at last he admitted it to himself. Wind. The one factor that lay at the heart of long range shooting. Wind, varying in strength as it came across the 600 yard heath that was the Century Range. And now, shooting as he would be across a bay, across 600 yards of water . . . wind that would be gusting, coming in sudden squalls.

And just for a moment he had to admit it. There was really very little chance.

33

It seemed a hell of a way.

Eight-thirty a.m., one-and-a-half hours to go, and he was sitting once again on the rocky point where he'd last been with Lela. He'd arrived a minute or two ago, having passed the scrub of the hillside, the trees of the man-made forest, and then the wall with its twin electrified fences.

Now it was maybe 200 yards away from him, the wall, and a little below. He was looking down slightly on the guardhouse built onto its end, right by the water's edge.

And 400 yards beyond, across water that was alternately dulled by wind, then bright, almost peeled by the yellow morning sunlight was the villa, with its crescent beach below.

A hell of a way.

He wasn't worried about the men in the guardhouse, about them hearing the shot when it came. Because of the wind, the same wind he would be fighting later on. Since last night it had backed, was now bringing the scent of dry earth and sage from the hills. And, more importantly, it was bringing the shriek of jet engines. This morning the bay was directly in the flightpath for Athens airport. Jetliners were coming in low, and by his watch they were landing roughly every six minutes.

No, he wasn't worried about the sound of the shot, not from the guardhouse a third of the way between rifle and target. Because he knew what the sound would be like there. One that was difficult to describe. Perhaps the nearest thing to it was the sound of a train, but a train without the noise of its engine or metal wheels on rails. A long sound, air on burnt air, a bullet building up its shock-wave as it travelled.

179

And the guards weren't going to hear that. Not with that other train travelling above, the 150-seater jetliner screaming its way down towards the airport.

He picked up the rifle once again. And once again sighted on the distant villa and beach. It looked better like that, a lot better, with the 12x magnification of the 'scope.

Except that the windows, every window he could see, were still shuttered and closed.

Eight-forty.

He began to worry.

That pulse, that faint thumping of blood, returned to his temples.

At eight-fifty, with just an hour and ten minutes to go, he saw movement through the 'scope. A door opened on the terrace of the villa. A maid came out, wearing a blue and white uniform, followed by another pushing a trolley. They began to lay a table, a long glass-topped table, with coffee cups and plates. Two coffee cups, two places only. One was visible, but the other was hidden behind a mass of trailing bougainvillaea, fat red and pink flowers, impossible to see through.

A fifty-fifty chance.

The terrace . . . For some reason he'd always counted on the beach as a target, perhaps because it fell so exactly at a range of 600 on the Michelin map. But at the same time he'd counted on the terrace too, calculated from map and eyesight that it was 30 yards back from the beach. And calculated also that with a High Velocity Round he'd have to add another $2\frac{1}{2}$ inches of elevation.

A High Velocity Round – an HVR. Faced now by the reality of the terrace and the beach below, he didn't want to think about HVRs. Because there was something he'd read somewhere, in a magazine or journal, about High Velocity Rounds . . . and impact.

The pumping grew stronger in his head.

But it would subside, he told himself, there was time for

it to subside. And he turned to his major problem now, the wind.

One of the first things he'd done on arriving at the rocky point was to look for flags. And there were three of them. Not as many as there would have been on the Century Range at Bisley, but still three.

The first, a yellow flag with a black monogram, was on the roof of the guardhouse at the end of the wall. The second, a similar flag, flew above the villa across the water. And the third, midway between them, was a yacht-marker, out in the bay.

The two outside flags, he saw, were steady, hanging down at about an angle of 45 degrees as they streamed. What in Bisley terms would be called Moderate. But the pennant out in the bay was gusting, gusting strongly, from what would be called Gentle to Fresh.

And as at Bisley, there was a technique for this. Not the technique normally used at 600 yards. But one used at far longer ranges, 900 to 1,200. The technique of the big money winners, the Queen's Prize Brigade. It involved shooting with both eyes open. Sighting through the 'scope with the right eye. And with the left watching the flags, seeing them not in clear focus but in blurred outline, yet at the same time knowing when they changed.

Because at the longest ranges you had to decide on a strength of wind. You had to take the average of the wind flags, watch them for some time, and settle for one particular strength that came more often than others. The rule rather than the exception.

But the difficulty was that, while you were waiting for the wind to come right, you had to keep the perfect aim.

Which meant more than the range-finding shots he'd fired back at the salt-pans. Far more. Eight shots he'd fired there altogether. Eight different times when he'd found the perfect aim, that moment, that tube that went out from his head towards the target. But now he had to find that moment and keep it, without a hair's breadth of doubt . . .

that moment of breath, of right thumb locked against cheek, of metal poised against metal, that *last* edge . . . keep it until the wind strength was exactly right.

Which was what won you the Queen's Prize, made you the one man among thousands.

And at Bisley perhaps you could do it. On the Stickle-down Range where there were perhaps five flags between you and the target. And where, yes, those flags could be varying from Gentle to Fresh. But never, as here, varying with such suddenness, the wind coming in such sudden gusts along a narrow bay. Because here, with the wind from 10 o'clock as it was now, the difference between Gentle and Fresh was, say, $4\frac{1}{2}$ inches on the wind gauge. Or, say, a shot hitting three feet adrift, to the left or the right.

Which was why an assassin, a professional, fired at 200 yards in a city street, where there was no wind.

He'd always known he'd have to have a sighter, a wind-sighter. And now he decided was the time to take it.

On the map he'd found a contour, a straight line over on the far side of the bay. And he'd seen it through the 'scope too, a smooth rock face a hundred yards to the right of the villa, but at the same range. There was also an aiming mark he'd found, a fault in the rock that seemed like a chicken's claw, three feet across.

He watched the wind-flags now, the pennant out in the water in particular. Watched it stream out suddenly as the water blurred around it, then keep steady at perhaps 60 degrees from the vertical.

And he decided to use that strength, Fresh, the one that came in the gusts. It was risky. It meant screwing more onto the wind-gauge, perhaps 6 inches, which could throw him four feet to the left in a lull. But the problem was that it was the only wind-strength he could count on, the gusts. They lasted perhaps ten, perhaps fifteen seconds each. There was no way of telling when they would come. But when they came they were steady.

He put 6 inches left on the wind-gauge, and waited for a plane.

It came, circling lazily out to sea. Then the shriek of its engines built up, the sun flamed on its silver belly.

He found the aim, the perfect aim, hair-lines crossed on the centre of the scar in the rock. He was relaxed, a half-breath easily held, that tiny metal edge waiting, just above his finger, in the gun. And with his left eye he caught the blur of the yacht-flag, saw it lift to the gust.

Then a clock, a microscopic clock without shake or movement, a drip of time in a vacuum, counted . . . one, two, three. He fired.

Rock chips sprang up to the left, a foot to the left, of his mark.

He thought about it for a moment. Then took off 1 inch, two clicks of wind, and waited.

At nine o'clock a tiny sound crossed the water, a handbell.

Through the 'scope he saw a woman come out onto the terrace, an elderly woman, lined and pale. She sat at the breakfast table, out in the open where he could see. And, while a maid poured coffee, she talked. To someone he couldn't see clearly. A man, hidden behind the bougainvillaea.

At twenty past nine she was finishing her second cup of coffee. The man still hadn't moved.

The pumping came back to Martin's head now. And to calm it, he clicked the safety catch off and worked the bolt. The empty sighter-shell ejected. The next round slid forward into the breech.

High Velocity Round. HVR . . . But still he wouldn't think about that, the thing he'd read in the magazine, about the impact.

The pumping grew worse.

Nine-thirty. And suddenly the man moved. For about twenty seconds Martin had a clear view of his face through the bougainvillaea blooms.

Yorgo Stefanides.

The thinning grey hair, the hawk nose, the glasses Lela had described to him. And the goitre scar, the cheap operation that had been performed years ago, Lela had said, years before he'd made his first hundred thousand *drachmes*. On the left side of his face, the side he never allowed to be photographed.

Yorgo Stefanides, the man who'd said last night, *Oh, and which one of your children d'you want killed? Pru or Simon?*

Martin's thumb hovered on the safety catch.

At nine-thirty-five one of the maids came down from the terrace to the beach. She carried a sun umbrella, a newspaper, and a cushion.

Just the one cushion.

Still a fifty-fifty chance.

She stuck the spike of the umbrella into the sand, placed the newspaper and cushion against it, then returned to the terrace. She passed the woman there, who made no move. But, from behind the bougainvillaea, the dark red blooms, Stefanides emerged.

He left the terrace and started down the steps to the beach.

And – Martin didn't understand the change that came then – out in the open suddenly . . . a man. A small man, stooped and nervous in white trousers and shirt. His hands nervous as they plucked at the collar of the shirt. His neck thin and creased there. And his eyes darting nervously behind glasses.

And suddenly too, in the 'scope around him . . . no longer just a range, a calculation, but a beach, dented sand, a bright-varnished morning, the smoke of summer on the water.

The man, Stefanides, looked round at it. He was still stooped, nervous, but for a moment pleased. He wiped the coffee from his lips with a handkerchief. He went over to the beach umbrella and lay back on the sand, his head rest-

184

ing on the cushion. One hand lifted up the newspaper and let it fall again.

Stefanides . . . in four parts . . . the hair-lines of the sight quartering him. The lines moved. They went up over his trousers, past his belt, to his shirt. Just below the open collar. Settled there.

And again Martin told himself about Pru and Simon, the phone call that was now only twenty minutes away.

Except that suddenly he could no longer see. He could see only the round that he'd slid forward into the breech . . . The High Velocity Round . . . And he could no longer keep away from what he knew:

The High Velocity Round, hitting a man's body, makes an entry wound the size of a knitting needle, and an exit wound the size of a football. At a maximum velocity of 4,000 feet per second, it kills hitting any part of a man's trunk, setting up a shock-wave that ruptures major organs.

Martin lifted his head from the sight. He told himself it was only to look round for a plane. There had to be a plane first.

The plane came a massive 707, slow and hawklike in the sky. It circled, leaving a web of burnt paraffin high up in the morning. Then started to come down, jets shrieking.

The sound built up.

Martin lowered his head to the sight again, found his position, pressed the safety catch forward. He took the shallow breaths, then the one that counted. He took first pressure, found the aim.

And with his left eye found the flag out in the bay . . . hanging down . . . kicking . . . streaming out.

And then not just the aim but the perfect aim, the vacuum, the tube that went out from him to the centre of that white shirt.

Exit wound the size of a . . .

Martin gasped, lost his breath.

The pumping started again, vicious, lurching in his head.

He broke aim.

The plane came on.

The flag, still steady, streaming out.

He breathed in again, found the aim again, easing it slowly to that point, that . . .

. . . *The size of a football.*

He fought against it, made himself concentrate only on the flag, on the sound of the plane that would soon pass. And that aim.

He fired.

And missed.

34

The spurt of sand was high, a yard high.

The man's arms came up. He sat up. But then was slow, confused by the plane, the sound of the plane. He looked round behind him at the sand, still slow.

Martin worked the bolt. And instinct now, blind instinct in the fading roar of the plane, the flap of the yacht flag in the bay, got him there.

A hole the size of a knitting needle.

The man lay there, arms flexed to the shock that had come and gone. And it was only under the arms that Martin saw, soaking away into the sand on either side, the blood, the matter.

The plane went. There was silence.

Up on the terrace the woman got to her feet. She leaned over the rail and called out to the man. Then she went away into the house, past the bougainvillaea.

The man lay there, on the beach.

Martin moved quickly. He stripped off the overalls and used them to wipe fingerprints from the gun. He wiped them from the cartridge cases, the charger, and the Michelin Guide.

He picked up the polythene sandwich bag he'd taken earlier from the gunman's apartment. He put the small transistor radio inside it, and his money, the rest of the *drachmas* that Halkis had given him. He slipped them inside the bathing trunks he was wearing, and went down among the rocks to the water.

35

He swam for a long time, swam and rested, his feet finding bottom as he kept close to the rocks. And the rocks were strange around him, white, gnarled and pitted like bones. The sea was strange too, warm, seemingly without substance. And the silence, that most of all.

But finally there were voices. Finally he emerged from the rocks to find a wide expanse of water, white under the sun, impossible to tell where it met the white of the sky. There were dots in the water, other swimmers. And beyond, Glyfada, its hotels and beaches.

He drew closer to the dots, children and old men in rubber swimming caps. He stayed among them for a while. And then, when a knot of them, a family, went back towards the beach, he joined them, keeping a little way behind.

The beach was grey, strewn with litter above the darker line of the waves. There were white duckboards leading up between rows of beach umbrellas and chairs. He followed the family up past them to a row of changing rooms, a shower. And he stayed under the shower a long while, washing the salt from his body.

He sat and dried himself next to a group of people sitting on a low wall. Their shouts, their dark laughing faces seemed far away. Every sound on the beach seemed far away. He turned away from it and slipped the polythene bag from his trunks. He took out the money. He went to a row of beach shops and bought a towel, a hat, sunglasses, beach clothes, and shoes. He joined a queue by a changing hut. He was handed a clothes hanger, and he went away to a booth. In its darkness he took the price tags from the new clothes and rubbed them against the booth wall until they were dirty. Then he arranged them on the hanger, keeping back the towel, the hat, and the sunglasses. He returned to the counter where he'd got the hanger, handed it back, and was given a numbered tab on a safety pin in exchange.

He went back to the beach and lay there. And every time a plane came over on its flightpath to the airport, he thought of that body lying on the beach around the point.

At eleven-thirty by his watch, a rustle went along the beach, a stiffening of alarm. And a voice, the same voice, harsh and Greek, echoed by transistor after transistor. A news announcement.

He pressed the radio to his ear and found words he understood, the Voice Of America.

. . . A second slaying, identical to the one that had ended Dr Grivela's life. The assassin had struck again.

The alarm on the beach spread. A few people looked round the point towards the next bay, whispered together, and left. But others came, others who hadn't heard the announcement on the bus-ride from Athens. And when now they heard, they stayed. Their children made them stay, shouting for their beach balls and their costumes. Gradually the beach reasserted itself. The groups thickened under the rows of umbrellas, and Martin moved to where they were thickest of all, lying quite still, keeping low.

At twelve noon, a second announcement.

New and dramatic information had now reached Athens police chief, Manoussakis. It was now definitely established that the assassin and Britisher Martin Baxter Raikes were not one and the same person. And while Raikes' role in the affair was still unclear . . .

Martin waited. Waited until four, when the dark figures on the beach began to drift back towards the showers. He followed them, feeling nothing, not even hunger, though he couldn't remember when he'd last eaten. The sounds around him were still distant, seemingly behind glass. He collected his clothes at the counter and went back once again to the darkness of the changing booth.

There was the fight, the usual panting fight at the bus-stop behind the beach. There was the long shuddering trip back to Athens, while bodies grew hotter and hotter around him, as though the day's swim had been in vain.

The haze, that dark clinker-haze of Athens, drew nearer. But greyer, darker suddenly, than Martin had ever seen it before. He watched it grow through the bus window, and he knew that by the time he got there, he'd have to have a story worked out. A hiding-place, somewhere he'd hidden until the news-announcement of four hours ago had been broadcast. It would have to be in an area of Athens he knew well, somewhere he'd stayed in the past few days. And there were other details he'd have to fill in too, stealing money, buying food, clothes.

By the time he reached the long line of bus-stops by the Zappion Gardens, he had the story clear in his mind. And he knew he could make it work, could carry it through. He walked between the gates of the gardens and along an asphalt path, making his way towards the Embassy, the concrete box-like building out on Vasilissis Sofias. Lela would be there, he knew, somewhere in the building. They would confront him with her, but he thought he could carry that through too. Though not from any of his doing, but from hers . . . Lela, Lela in that cage she'd talked about this morning, the smells she'd talked about, of paperwork, of power, of deodorisers . . . To Lela now he would just be part of that cage, of the interrogation. She would want it over, finished with.

And it was finished with, he suddenly realised. Because he reached the avenue, Vasilissis Sofias, where the sky was wide above him. And that metallic greyness that he'd seen before, that he'd thought was haze, he now realised was something else. For the first time since he'd been in Athens, clouds were edging in to cover the city. High, thick, and grey, a solid line, they brought almost an English sky.

He walked on. A garden, a green garden under beech trees, was suddenly close. A garden where little girls in party dresses left small footprints on a lawn. Where the sound of a piano came from inside a house. Where that piano stopped ... And he was there again, holding Shirley close. She was reaching out towards the keyboard again, and the little girls were dancing on.

He was there.

He was going back.